D0099725

Hillsboro Public Library
Hillsboro, OR
A member of Washington County
COOPERATIVE LIBRARY SERVICES

LOVE AND F1RST SIGHT

A NOVEL BY
JOSH SUNDQUIST

Little, Brown and Company
New York   Boston

Also by Josh Sundquist

Just Don't Fall

We Should Hang Out Sometime

This book is a work of fiction. Names, characters, places, and incidents are the product of the author's imagination or are used fictitiously. Any resemblance to actual events, locales, or persons, living or dead, is coincidental.

Copyright © 2017 by Josh Sundquist

All rights reserved. In accordance with the U.S. Copyright Act of 1976, the scanning, uploading, and electronic sharing of any part of this book without the permission of the publisher is unlawful piracy and theft of the author's intellectual property. If you would like to use material from the book (other than for review purposes), prior written permission must be obtained by contacting the publisher at permissions@hbgusa.com. Thank you for your support of the author's rights.

Little, Brown and Company

Hachette Book Group
1290 Avenue of the Americas, New York, NY 10104
Visit us at lb-teens.com

Little, Brown and Company is a division of Hachette Book Group, Inc.
The Little, Brown name and logo are trademarks of Hachette Book Group, Inc.

The publisher is not responsible for websites (or their content) that are not owned by the publisher.

First Edition: January 2017

Library of Congress Cataloging-in-Publication Data

Names: Sundquist, Josh, author.
Title: Love and first sight / by Josh Sundquist.
Description: First edition. | New York : Little, Brown and Company, 2017. | Summary: "Sixteen-year-old blind teen Will Porter undergoes an experimental surgery that enables him to see for the first time, all while navigating a new school, new friends, and a crush"— Provided by publisher.
Identifiers: LCCN 2015044093| ISBN 9780316305358 (hardcover) | ISBN 9780316305334 (ebook) | ISBN 9780316305372 (library edition ebook)
Subjects: | CYAC: Blind—Fiction. | People with disabilities—Fiction. | High Schools—Fiction. | Schools—Fiction.
Classification: LCC PZ7.1.S866 Lo 2017 | DDC [Fic]—dc23
LC record available at http://lccn.loc.gov/2015044093

10 9 8 7 6 5 4 3 2 1

LSC-H

Printed in the United States of America

3361405783118 1

To Ashley Sundquist—
this time I can use your real last name

CHAPTER 1

Vice Principal Larry Johnston extends his hand.

To clarify: I don't see this. I hear the swish of his shirtsleeve.

"Nice to meet you, William."

The fabric sound plays again—the hand retracting.

"I'm sorry, I guess you can't do that now, can you? You probably want to feel my face?"

He grabs my arm and smacks my palm against his cheek, knocking me off balance so I have to step into the musk of his aftershave.

"Where do you normally start? Eyes? Nose? Mouth?"

He shifts my fingers across the front of his face with each suggestion. His skin is rough and pockmarked, like the outside of an orange.

"No, actually, I don't do that," I say, pulling my hand away. "I identify people based on their voices."

"And...also..." I add. I can't resist.

"Yes?" he asks, all eager to please.

"Well, I don't usually touch faces, but I am gifted with a heightened sense of smell that allows me to recognize a person's pheromones, which are concentrated just below the ear, so if you wouldn't mind...?"

I touch my pointer finger to my nose.

His excitement drops. "Oh...you want to...smell... my ear?"

"Pheromones are like faces to me. Only if it's not too much trouble, sir."

"Oh, no, no trouble at all. I just...No trouble, certainly I would like to accommodate you."

He steps close enough that I can feel the heat of his body, which is a signal that (a) he is falling for it—sighted people always do, the suckers—and (b) I've taken the joke far enough. I don't actually want my nose anywhere near his old-guy earwax, after all.

"Mr. Johnston, I'm kidding." I hold a hand up to stop him. It sinks deep into fat rolls, presumably around his midsection. I hope. "A joke, sir. I don't want to smell your ear."

When I pull my hand away, I wonder if it leaves a visible handprint or even fingerprints in his squishy flesh. I've heard that happens when you press an open palm against a soft surface like sand, dough, or wet paint.

"Oh, right, yes." He lets out a forced chuckle that sounds like a wheezy smoker's cough. "A joke. Yes. Very funny."

Mr. Johnston's voice is deep and grizzly. If you listen carefully, you learn that a particular set of vocal cords produces audio vibrations unlike any other in the world. Voices are the fingerprints of sound.

"Shall we head to your first class?" he asks.

He grabs my arm from behind and starts to push me out of the front office. I'm sure he thinks it's helpful to lead me like that, but I instinctively swap our positions so I am holding his arm instead.

"I'd prefer we walk like this," I say. Now I'm in control. I can let go at any time.

"Yes, all right, that's fine," he says.

I've spent most of my sixteen years around other blind and visually impaired people, so this is the first time I've actually had to execute a Hines Break in real life. Fortunately, Mrs. Chin made me practice so many times I could do it automatically with Mr. Johnston. The main purpose of this little arm reversal is that it puts me in charge. To put it in dating terms, I can now be the dumper rather than the dumpee.

I've heard the horror stories: Blind people standing on street corners waiting for a crosswalk light to change, only to have a well-meaning but annoying stranger come up from behind, grab their arm, and say (overly loud, of course, because they always assume we are all deaf, too) "LET ME HELP YOU!" and shove them across a street they were not intending to cross. And then the stranger lets go and disappears into the void ("YOU'RE WEL-COME!"), leaving the blind person stranded on an unknown street corner.

I feel the floor change from the carpet of Mr. Johnston's office to the hard tile of the hallway as I follow him through the doorway.

"Can we start at the front door?" I ask. "That's where I'll be coming in each morning, I assume."

"Isn't that where you came in today?" he asks.

"Yes, but my mom took me from there to your office."

"Well, then, simply imagine that instead of turning into the office, you walked in this direction toward the stairwell, and you'll be on your way to first period."

He starts to walk, presumably toward said stairwell. But I stand still, gripping his arm tightly so he is forced to stop. (Behold the mighty power of the Hines Break!)

"It doesn't work like that. I can't..." I drift off.

I hate sentences that start with "I can't."

But as it happens, I was born completely blind, so one thing I truly can't do is imagine an overhead map and then make up different routes or shortcuts. I can walk from A to B, yes, but only if I memorize a list of actions: How many steps to take and when to turn and then how many more steps to take before I'm there. I can sniff odors like a bloodhound and echolocate sounds like a bat, but it is simply impossible for me to infer a new route using my imagination.

"Look, Mr. Johnston, can we just start at the front door, please? That would be much easier for me."

4

"Are you sure you don't want us to assign you a full-time aide? The state would gladly pay—"

"I know, I know, but that's not why I transferred here. Having a babysitter walk me around school every day is not going to help my street cred."

Honestly, it's not just about my street cred. I transferred because I want to prove that I can live independently in the sighted world. No dependence on charity. No *neediness*.

My parents sent me off to the school for the blind back when I was little. Right after the Incident. It was "for my own good," to "protect me," and blah, blah, blah. But if I want to eventually land my dream job, to make a name for myself as the Stevie Wonder of journalism, it's not going to happen within the confines of the blind bubble— excuse me, the *visually impaired community*. I have to go mainstream.

I hear Mr. Johnston sigh. But when he speaks, there's a hint of sympathy in his voice, as if maybe he was once young enough to care about his own street cred. Or maybe he still does. "Very well, William, to the front door we shall go."

He guides me there.

"First I need to get my bearings," I say.

"Well, the door is in front of you, the wall is beside—"

"No," I say, pulling my iPhone out of my pocket. "I literally need compass bearings."

My compass app tells me I will enter the building facing west.

Got it: west. (Seriously, how did anyone get by before talking smartphones?)

"Mr. Johnston, let's head to English. If possible," I say, "please walk in a straight line and tell me when we are going to change directions."

"Very well."

We walk twelve steps west, twenty-three steps south, and then turn west again. Mr. Johnston tells me we are at the base of a stairwell. I hear footsteps rushing by on both sides of us, students in a hurry to get to first period.

Up to this point, I've kept my white cane folded in my back pocket. No use drawing attention to myself if I don't have to. But I'll feel safer using the cane on stairs than relying on a vice principal with a lifetime total of three minutes' experience guiding a blind person.

I pull it out and, with a quick flick of my wrist, snap the whole thing open. People have told me this looks like a *Star Wars* lightsaber turning on. That's not a particularly helpful description for me, though. Which also makes me wonder why it's called a "white cane" in the first place, since the people who use them can't see its color.

Anyway, I reach out for the handrail, but my fingers grab something soft instead. A body part. Chest level. *Boob alert.*

"Oh, my God, I am SO sorry, I tooootally didn't see you there," says a female voice.

That's what a white cane will do for you: Not only can

you get away with copping a feel, the girl assumes it was her fault and *apologizes* for it. Let me assure you, random girl, you have nothing to be sorry about. Completely my fault. And my pleasure.

"No problem," I tell her. "I didn't *see* you, either."

She doesn't laugh. She is already gone before I say it, the sound of her footsteps lost in the shuffle.

I hate that. When I discover I'm talking to someone who has already walked away. Feels like when you tell some long story into your cell phone and you wonder why the person has been silent for a while and then you realize the call was dropped at some point.

At the top of this flight of stairs, Mr. Johnston tells me we are going to turn 180 degrees and go up another. I continue to climb with one hand on the rail and the other pencil-gripping my cane as it surveys the next step. Once we've reached the second floor, I fold the cane and return it to my right back pocket. I can feel how the fabric of my jeans has stretched around that shape, the form of my folded cane. For the first time, I wonder if this distortion is visible.

Footsteps drop all around us like a heavy rainstorm. As Mr. Johnston guides me eighteen steps east through the crowded hallway, he shouts, "Clear a path, people! Blind student coming through! Blind student coming through!"

Wow, thanks, Mr. Johnston. I'm sure this is gaining me *so* many popularity points at my new school. My election as Prom King is now all but assured.

We pause at the door to my classroom so I can dictate the directions into my phone. ("Enter building, walk twelve steps west, turn south, walk twenty-three steps...") I'll have Siri read them back to me after school until I've got the route memorized.

"Attention, everyone!" Mr. Johnston says as soon as we cross the threshold. His voice sounds pleased, maybe even surprised, by its ability to silence the chattering room. "This is Will, a student who has transferred to our school this year. He's blind."

Perhaps because this is English class, he adds a helpful definition of the word: "He can't see anything... nothing at all." He pauses to allow the gravity of my tragic situation to sink in. "Life is very difficult for him. Please offer him your assistance whenever you can, because—"

"You know I'm still standing right beside you, right?" I interrupt.

There's a snort of laughter from the students, and Mr. Johnston's arm stiffens against my fingers. It's probably unwise to make fun of your guide, the guy who has the capacity to lead you, say, directly into a brick wall. But come on, I don't need eyesight to know his speech was making the entire room squirm.

"Yes, William, I—I..." he stammers.

"Listen, sorry, I appreciate your help," I say. "Can you guide me to the teacher?"

"I'm right here, William. Or do you prefer Will?" asks a female voice standing maybe two arm lengths away.

"Most people call me Will," I say.

"I'm Mrs. Everbrook. I'll take it from here, Larry."

"Very well," says Mr. Johnston. "William…er, Will, I will meet you at the end of this period to escort you to your next class."

He shuffles out.

"The bell hasn't rung yet, boys and girls," says Mrs. Everbrook. "Until it does, you can go back to texting underneath your desks and I'll go back to pretending I don't notice you have your cell phones out of your lockers."

Unlike Mr. Johnston's, hers sounds like a voice people listen to.

"Will, there's a desk open immediately to your right," she says. I sit. She continues, "I was told you'd be in my class, so I've already talked to the library, and they can get you all the books we'll be reading this term. Do you prefer braille or audiobooks?"

"Braille, please. And thank you. For talking to the library, I mean."

"No problem. Whatever else you need, just ask. I'm happy to help. Otherwise, you get the same treatment as everyone else. This is Honors English, and I expect honors-level work from you."

"Thank you," I say. "That's very nice."

"You may change that opinion after I grade your first paper. No one has ever accused me of being nice. But I try to be fair."

"Then I hope this request appeals to your sense of

fairness: I type notes into my phone during class so that it can read them back to me later. Is that all right?"

"Fine by me. Just don't let me catch you texting your girlfriend during class."

If I had a girlfriend, I think.

I dated several girls back at the school for the blind. But it would be different here. Dating a girl without a visual impairment, I couldn't help but be beholden to her. Dependent. *Needy.*

"Oh, no girlfriend, huh?" she asks.

"How can you tell?"

"Your inability to see doesn't stop your face from speaking what's on your mind."

"Hmmm. Well, I did meet a girl downstairs this morning. She seemed nice."

"Anything else?"

"She was also very apologetic."

"I don't care about the personality of your crush, Will. I mean any other accommodations you need?"

"I wear one earbud in my ear."

"Because?"

"My phone reads everything on-screen to me—the names of apps, the selections on menus, all that. The earbud will let me hear the phone without disturbing the class."

"How about that? Anyway, it's fine. You can use your headphones. Just don't—"

"Let you catch me listening to music in class? Got it."

"I was actually going to say anything other than country."

"What?"

"Don't let me catch you listening to anything other than country music during my class."

"I'm not into country, so I guess I'll just be listening to you teach."

"I like you, Will. I think we're going to get along just fine."

Which is good, because it turns out I have her again for third period. And that class begins with a major social disaster.

CHAPTER 2

In between each class, Mr. Johnston takes me by my locker so I can learn the route from each classroom. On my locker, the school has replaced the standard spinning numerical padlock with one that opens when you press in a certain combination of up, down, right, and left on the face of the lock. Like unlocking a cheat-code with a controller on an old video game system.

On the way to third period, Mr. Johnston asks why I'm not wearing sunglasses.

"What do you mean?" I ask, playing dumb.

"Well, you know, many individuals with, um, your condition wear sunglasses. Are your people maybe sensitive to sunlight?"

"I think you are getting us confused with vampires," I say, and leave it at that.

He does his fake laugh-snort, but I know he's still desperately curious. Probably also wants to know if I can have dreams. Whatever. He can Google it later.

I don't wear sunglasses for the same reason I left the school for the blind: The vast majority of the world doesn't wear sunglasses indoors, and I want to fit in. I'm not trying to fake anything, but there's no reason to call attention to what makes me different.

I ask Mr. Johnston to leave me at the doorway to Mrs. Everbrook's classroom, and then I walk to the same desk I sat in during Honors English. I already know the route, after all.

When the bell rings, Mrs. Everbrook addresses the class.

"Boys and girls, welcome to journalism. This is unlike any other class you will take during high school. We don't have textbooks. We don't have tests. We don't have lectures. We work together to write, edit, print, and distribute a newspaper, and you will be graded based on how well you contribute to that goal."

I hear quick footsteps as someone walks in late.

"Do you have a note for being tardy, Xander?"

"No."

I recognize the sound of his voice from the morning announcements that played on the television in English during first period.

"Then don't let it happen again." She continues to the class, "As I was saying. In my English classes, you all are always asking me how diagramming sentences will help you in the real world. Well, I'll let you in on a little secret: It probably won't. But everything we do in *this* class *is* real world. We're running a real business funded by the real money from the ads we sell. Our end product is a real print publication. Plus, as the school's most esteemed group of student journalists from each grade, some of you will play a role in producing the morning announcements show at the start of every day. You can even audition to be one of the hosts if you want to try to end the three-year streak of our tardy friend Xander and his cohost, Victoria."

I hear her get up from her desk and step in front of it.

"This is your staff handbook and our publishing schedule for the year. Take one and pass it on."

Something heavy thuds onto a desk several arm lengths in front of me. Sheets slide off, and I hear another thud, this time a little closer, on the desk in front of me. Paper is removed, and the pile hits my desk. It's not like I can do much with a printed handbook, but I don't want to stand out for not taking one, so I tug at the top sheet, and it pulls with it a stapled packet about ten pages thick. I pick up the remainder of the stack, which is big and heavy enough to require both hands, rotate in my seat, and drop it on the desk behind mine.

Only, there's no thud. I suppose if you calculated the acceleration due to gravity, you'd find that the time the stack traveled to reach the floor was inconsequentially longer than it would have had to travel to reach a desk, but in that millisecond, I live a thousand lives and die a thousand social deaths. The thump when the pages finally hit the ground—since apparently I am at the end of a row—is followed by the racket of pages bouncing and sliding off the pile.

The class erupts in laughter. After all, they don't yet know that I can't see. If they did, they probably wouldn't find it funny.

"Calm down, everyone, all right, that's enough," says Mrs. Everbrook. She's coming toward me, and she squats to rake up the pages. "That could happen to anyone on his first day at a new school. This is Will. He's...well...as you can tell, he's...a transfer student. So be nice to him."

She sets a soft hand on my shoulder as she walks by and returns to her drill sergeant voice.

"Now, some of you"—she pauses and repeats herself, projecting to various sections of the room—"*some* of you took this class because you thought it sounded easy...or maybe even fun. Well, it's only fun if you like hard work, because it certainly ain't easy. And yes, I know *ain't* isn't proper grammar, but we ain't in English class anymore. This here's *journalism*. So if you're looking for an easy A, go to your guidance counselor today and switch to one of those 'fun' electives"—she makes *fun* sound downright offensive—"like finger painting or basket weaving or yearbook or whatever they are offering these days."

There are some snickers, but they are interrupted by a shriek from directly across the room.

"Stop staring!" shouts a female voice.

I hear a chair push back with a screech before someone runs by me and out into the hall, crying.

"All right, boys and girls, I guess I should have told you this earlier, but I was trying to respect Will's privacy.

Seems I made a mistake. Anyway, Will, our new transfer student, is blind."

There are several loud gasps. It's a stronger reaction than I'm used to.

"Don't worry, people, it's not contagious," I say.

But no one laughs.

"All righty, then, big first day," says Mrs. Everbrook. "I guess this is as good a time as any to let you all know that Victoria is going to be our editor in chief this year. Her duties will include, among other things, chasing down crying staff members. Victoria, would you please see to it that Cecily is all right?"

"No problem," says a voice I assume belongs to Victoria. She marches efficiently out of the room.

Mrs. Everbrook approaches my desk and says quietly, "Will, you were staring at Cecily."

"I thought we just established—"

"Yes, I know that, but she didn't. So she thought you were staring."

"And that made her cry?" I ask.

"I'm sure you've heard before that some people are sensitive about being stared at," says Mrs. Everbrook. "Cecily is . . . she's just one of those people. Do you understand?"

"I guess."

But I don't, not really. I feel my face getting hot, and I wonder if the other students can see the temperature change on my skin. Are they all staring at me right now?

Mom *hates* it when people stare at me. Especially when I was little, before the Incident and thus before I went to the school for the blind. She would take me grocery shopping or whatever, and I'd be walking down the aisle with my little tiny white cane in one hand, the other holding her by the wrist—she always insisted I grip her like that instead of holding hands so that I would grow up comfortable with being guided—and some other kid would look at me funny, and Mom would go all Mama Bear, roaring, "If you stare, you'll go blind, too!" And the kid would run off crying.

She's always been that way. Overprotective. Not for my sake as much as for hers. I think she wants my life to be easy because it will make her life easy. She can't let me fail because then everyone would think *she* failed as a mother.

So that's why she yells at people for staring. And why she tries to make me "fit in" so they don't stare in the first place. She's actually always wanted me to wear sunglasses in public.

And I guess she was right about that one, because here I am now, making some girl cry because she thought *I* was staring at *her*. Wouldn't have happened if I had been wearing the glasses.

• • •

After journalism is lunch. Mr. Johnston invites me to eat with him in the staff lounge, but I decline. He deposits me in the cafeteria, where I stand holding my cane in one hand and a bag lunch in the other. Is the entire room staring at me? Or am I invisible to them? I don't know. All I have to go on is the sound of hundreds of people talking at once, the voices blending together so that I can't pick out individual conversations.

The noise of the cafeteria is not unlike the *smell* of the cafeteria. It combines the long list of foods that are being consumed today, or have been consumed in this room at some point in the past, into one overpowering yet nondescript odor that welcomes you like a smack across the face.

I walk forward until my cane clinks against the metal legs of a chair. Further cane taps determine that the chair is already pulled out from a circular lunch table.

"Excuse me, is anyone sitting at this table?" I ask the void.

In return, I get nothing but the chattering voices of the room.

"No one?"

No response.

So I sit. But instead of a chair, my butt makes contact with another animate life-form. A pair of legs, I think. I jump.

"What the—" I holler, completely startled.

"AHHHH!" comes from the owner of the legs.

I drop my cane.

Mrs. Chin always said that a blind person losing a cane is like a sighted person dropping a flashlight and having it turn off after it hits the ground in a dark room. Not only will I have to find the cane, I will have to do so on hands and knees because I've lost the very thing that normally helps me detect lost objects.

"Dude, let me get that for you," says the owner of the legs. With enviable quickness, he retrieves the cane and places it in my hand. "There you go. Sorry, bro. So sorry. That was majorly awkward and totally my fault."

"It's all right. But, I mean, did you hear me ask if anyone—"

"Yeah, yeah, I heard you. Like I said, I'm sorry, it was totally messed up not to answer you. I just...I don't know, I saw you walking over here and froze. Look, you wanna sit down? The chair next to me is empty."

I hesitate.

He says, "I swear, no surprise occupants."

I sit down. "Okay, sure, thanks."

"I'm Nick, by the way."

"Will."

I reach my hand toward his voice, and he shakes it. (Side note, Mr. Johnston: I am perfectly capable of shaking hands.)

I hear more people sit down at the table.

"So, Will, before we have any more awkward butt contact, I should introduce you to my friends," says Nick. He's loud. Loud enough that I assume much of the cafeteria is forced to listen to his nasally proclamations.

"*Friend.* Singular," says a female voice to my right.

"I'm retracting my friendship with you, so you've only got one left."

"That's Ion. We've been feuding recently," Nick says to me. "Argument about time travel. Won't bore you with the details. She's just pissed because she knows I'm right."

"*Please.* Another dimension is the only explanation that—" says Ion.

"If you had the technology to travel in time, you could obviously figure out how to remain—" interrupts Nick.

"WHOA, WHOA," I say, overpowering their voices. "Too much talking at once. You are welcome to bore me with the details, but at least take turns, please."

"Okay," says Nick. "SparkNotes version: A while ago some geeks made a permanent monument out of stone or whatever that was inscribed with an invitation to a party that would be thrown in honor of time travelers from the future. The idea was that millions of years from now, when time travel exists, the stone invitation thingy would still be around, and humans of the future would see it and travel back in time to attend the party. The only problem was—"

"No one showed up," interrupts Ion. She continues at what I assume is the maximum words per minute a human is capable of pronouncing without compromising diction or dropping syllables. "From the future, I mean. But that doesn't mean that time travel will never be invented. Because anyone who has consumed *any* science fiction knows that there are paradoxes created when you travel back in time and meddle with the past. So it stands to reason that if humans *did* travel back in time, they would be entering a time line of a parallel dimension. The first dimension would be the way things are now, without time travel. That's where we are living, obviously. The next dimension would be the version of reality that was created when they traveled back in time. So maybe a bunch of time travelers attended the party; it just happened in a different dimension."

"Which obviously makes no sense," says Nick. "Because—"

"It is the *only* explanation that makes—"

"Wow. So, Ion? Is that your given name?" I ask, trying to change the subject to something less volatile.

"Yeah," she says.

"No!" says Nick. "Tell him the truth!"

"Why do you always have to tell people this story?" she asks.

"It's endearing!" says Nick.

"It's embarrassing. That's why my parents started calling me Ion in the first place."

"So your given name is..." I prompt.

"It's Hermione, all right?" says Ion, eliciting peals of laughter from Nick. "Yes, like in *Harry Potter*. Only my parents were living under a rock and had never even heard of the books. It was, like, my great-aunt's name or something. Anyway, after the first movie came out, it didn't take long for my parents to get tired of hearing jokes about how my baby talk was probably a spell I was casting."

"I can see how that would get old," I say.

"Right, so my parents decided to make a nickname out of Hermione. They couldn't use Her or Nee, obviously, so they used the middle sound: Ion."

"I like it," I say. "It's unique."

"Thanks," says Ion.

Nick says, "Will, I still feel bad about earlier, and I want to make it up to you by serving as your eyes at this table. Cool?"

"I guess."

"So here's something you should know about Ion: She's like the nerd chick in teen movies who, if she brushed her hair and put on girl clothes, would suddenly be transformed into, like, a smoking-hot babe."

References to visual components of cinema are meaningless to me, of course, but I appreciate Nick's effort.

Ion says, "You realize I'm sitting right here, right?"

"I get that a lot, too," I say to Ion.

"About being transformed into a smoking-hot babe?" asks Nick.

"No, people talking about me like I'm not here," I say.

A new voice says, "Speaking of people who are actually sitting right here, Ion's boyfriend is sitting right here, too, and he's about to beat the crap out of you, Nick." It's male, positioned opposite me, in between Ion and Nick. The voice is deep and resonant, almost musical.

"My bad," says Nick. "Will, I would like to introduce Whitford."

"Pleasure to meet you," says Whitford.

"You too," I say.

"Now, based on his name and the sound of his voice," continues Nick, "you're probably thinking Whitford is a white dude, right?"

"Well, I...I mean..." I stammer.

"It's cool. I always say what everyone is thinking but knows isn't appropriate to share out loud," says Nick. "Obviously Whitford sounds white. I mean, jeez, it's right there in his name. Whitford. WHITE-ford. But no, good sir, our friend Whitford is a genuine African American."

"This is uncomfortable for everyone and amusing for no one," says Whitford dryly.

"Think of him as a young Tiger Woods," adds Nick.

"*So* uncomfortable..." says Whitford.

"Except without the girl addiction. And dressed even *more* preppy," concludes Nick.

Sighted people are always doing this: Imagining they are translating vision into words for me, but they're really just describing one image by comparing it to another image, neither of which I have a point of reference for.

"And finally, I'm your host, Nick, a clever lad with mild premature baldness and the potential to either graduate valedictorian or drop out of high school. I haven't decided which yet."

"Nice to meet you all," I say.

"So how does a wacky gang like us end up as friends?" continues Nick. "I mean, this lunch table packs the sort of uncanny diversity you normally only see in TV commercials, am I right?"

"I don't watch commercials," I say.

"I don't, either," says Nick. "Thank God for DVR."

"No, I meant because—"

"I know what you meant, Will. Jeez, I thought we were at a point in our relationship where we could joke about things like that. I mean, after the intimacy of our initial physical contact—"

"Okay, whatever," I say. "I'll bite: How did all of you become friends?"

"Will, I don't want to make you nervous or anything," says Nick. "But you are currently seated with the Toano High School varsity academic quiz team, defending district champions and regional runner-ups!"

"Varsity?" I ask.

"No," says Whitford. "We're just a club. Nick always tries to make us sound like a sport because he's bitter about being born white, which means he lacks the natural athletic prowess stereotypically associated with a black man such as myself."

"Don't kid yourself, Whitford," says Nick. "You're a nerd, too."

"I'm a geek," says Whitford. "There's a difference."

"Well, thanks for letting me eat with you guys," I say,

realizing I have forgotten all about the lunch Mom carefully packed into braille-labeled Tupperware containers. "I'm new here, and I don't know anyone, so—"

"Hey, it's the least we could do," says Nick. "I shouldn't have been silent like that when you asked if there was anyone here. I mean, we're the academic quiz team. Answering questions is what we do."

But even the defending district champion academic quiz team would have trouble answering the number of questions I get from my parents after school.

CHAPTER 3

I'm waiting at the edge of the curb.

"Right here, William!"

It's Mom's voice, startlingly close. Maybe two arm lengths. Yet I'm unable to hear the familiar hum of our family station wagon.

My hand reaches for the door handle, but my fingers jam into hard metal. I press my palm against the car, searching for the lever.

This goes on for a second or two, and I still can't seem to find it.

Mom says, "Surprise, honey! New car!"

She claps a few times, as if I need additional auditory cues that she is excited. She's been doing that since I was a baby, going out of her way to signal excitement to me when it just ends up making me feel like a toddler. And I think she still sees me that way: the same little boy who went off to boarding school in kindergarten. She doesn't realize I'm grown up now.

"We got a Teslaaaaaaaaaa!" Mom says in a talk-show-announcer voice.

Apparently I'm supposed to be excited about this, but mostly I just feel dumb because, like, where's the door handle? I grope around for a while, and finally she notices my struggle.

"Just a little to the left, honey," she says, returning to her normal voice.

I locate it and climb in.

"Your father finished early in the operating room today, so we just went out and bought it!" exclaims Mom.

"It was the new less-expensive model, and it will reduce our carbon footprint and save on gas," says Dad. "And we can install a bike rack on the roof."

"What do you think? You like it?" asks Mom.

I sniff as I feel us silently accelerating away from the school.

"It certainly smells like a new car," I say. "But it's electric?"

"That's right," confirms Dad in the same voice he'd use to describe his favorite road bike. "Zero emissions, no fuel costs, and it can run for hundreds of miles on a single charge. Cool, huh?"

It's so weird to hear your parents describe something as "cool."

"Well...yeah," I say. But really, it's not cool.

"You don't sound happy, Will," says Dad. "When you

were little, you used to love mechanical gadgets. I thought you would be impressed."

"Oh, no, I am," I stammer. "I mean, zero emissions, that's great."

"But?" prods Dad.

I came home to prove that I could live outside the blind bubble without burdening anyone. But here I am, already being an inconvenience.

"Well, electric motors are *silent*."

When I walk to an intersection, I decide whether it's safe to cross by listening to the flow of traffic. If an electric car is coming down the street, I might as well be blind *and* deaf.

Mom says, "Don't worry. I told the salesman—didn't you hear me ask him, Henry?"

"Yes, dear," says Dad.

"I said to him, 'Sir, I have a son who is visually impaired. Will he be safe with this vehicle?' And the salesman told me, 'Ma'am, don't worry, I don't think his condition will affect the performance of the air bags or the seat belts. And if your son is sitting in the driveway playing'"—Jeez. Sounds like she described me as a child or something—"'it comes with a'... Hold on, I wrote this down." She smooths out a slip of folded paper. "The engine emits a 'sound like a gentle breeze' that should alert pedestrians to the car."

I say, "I was standing at the curb just now, and I didn't hear any gentle breeze."

After an awkward pause, Mom asks, "So how was your first day?"

"It was okay, I guess."

Parents ask you questions about your life the way police officers interrogate subjects on TV cop shows. No matter how much information you provide, they will always follow up a hundred times with slightly reworded questions. So you might as well give short answers and let them pry out the facts incrementally so they feel they are making conversational progress.

"Was Vice Principal Johnston helpful? He seemed so nice," says Mom.

"Sure," I say.

"What about journalism class? You're such a good writer, you must've had a ball."

I think about third period—the girl crying and running out of the room, my burning-hot face.

"Totally."

"Oh, good. I knew you would love it!" says Mom.

I feel us slow down, turn right, and then slow down again to wait for the gate to rise so we can enter our neighborhood. Despite how far away my mom imagines the "other side of town" to be, Toano, Kansas, is actually quite small. It only seems large to her because when she looks at it, all she sees is the giant divide created by this gate.

"Did you make any friends?" asks Dad.

"A few," I say.

"Nice kids?" he asks.

"Not bad."

"Right on," says Dad, a little too loudly.

My father is an uptight surgeon. He fools no one by using phrases he thinks are cool.

"Did your new friends like your sweater?" asks Mom. "It looks so perfect on you!"

"They failed to mention it," I say.

"Was it tough getting around?" asks Mom. "So much new territory. I mean, after ten years at the school for the blind—"

"It was okay. Mrs. Chin trained me well."

Mrs. Chin was the "orienteering and mobility" guide at the school for the blind, where I used to go. She taught us how to walk with an adult-size white cane, how to cross an intersection, how to orient in a new building using cardinal directions—almost everything we needed to know about living independently. I can't say for sure since we didn't talk about that kind of stuff, but I think Mrs. Chin was Chinese American. I assume so because I once heard a joke about a fat person having "more chins than a Chinese phone book."

It's amazing how jokes can teach you the things people *think* but are too polite to say aloud, prejudices I assume other kids absorb with the help of their eyes—racism, sexism, and the like. In the case of Mrs. Chin, I figured she was probably Chinese after I heard the phone book line. In fact, that very same joke also taught me that fat people have multiple chins. Why this is, I don't know. I mean, why chins? Why not extra cheeks? Or foreheads?

"You didn't meet any mean kids, did you?" Mom asks.

I know why she's asking. It's the same reason she and Dad sent me off to the school for the blind in the first place: the Incident.

It happened back when I was around five years old.

My best friend at the time was a boy from the neighborhood named Alexander. He always helped me when I couldn't do something. He'd explain a playground or take my turn for me in a game. Like that day, when we were playing Candy Land at the kitchen table. Alexander offered to move my piece for me. I would flip a card, then he would say which color it was and move me down the rainbow road to that square. We played a few rounds, and he kept winning every single time. I was annoyed, but I didn't complain, because Mom had said I had to be nice to him.

Then Mom came into the kitchen.

"Will, what color is your piece?" she asked.

"Red," I answered, proud to be able to answer such a question.

"Why is your piece still at the starting area?"

"It's not. Alexander moves it for me when it's my turn."

Her head swiveled to face Alexander so abruptly that I heard the rustle of her collar.

She didn't speak, but something about her head swivel must have made Alexander know he should say something. "Who cares? He can't see the pieces anyway!"

"How dare you—" blurted Mom.

"He doesn't even know what *red* is. Do you, Will? Huh? What does red look like?"

He was right, of course. I didn't know.

Mom snapped, "You've just been moving your own piece? On both your and Will's turns?"

"Yeah. So? He can't see the board!" Alexander said defiantly. "It doesn't matter where his piece is."

Mom sent him home. I never saw him again.

That day, two things happened: First, I learned it was dangerous to rely on anyone other than myself. And second, my parents decided it would be better for me to enroll in the school for the blind rather than the neighborhood elementary school. I didn't particularly want to leave home. But Mom and Dad said I would have more fun at a place where everyone was more like me.

They were right, I guess. And yet . . .

Attending the school for the blind, day after day, year after year, it felt like I was trapped in the starting area of real life. Sure, I was safe there. But I was also bored. I wanted to break free and move forward on the winding rainbow road of life. I might not be able to experience those colors the way some people did, but I believed I could still make it. Make it, you know, to the Candy Castle. Or whatever. But for that to happen, I had to at least start playing the game.

CHAPTER 4

By my second day at my new school, I know all my routes. No more of Mr. Johnston moving me from class to class. I'm free to go as I please.

Before Honors English, Mrs. Everbrook asks me to come over to her desk. Usually, people assume it's rude to make the blind kid walk across the room, but blindness is an eye problem, not a leg problem. Mrs. Everbrook clearly gets this, which I appreciate.

"Listen, Will, the librarians have everything on my syllabus ordered for you, but it will be about a week before the small forest of literature gets here."

Braille books, I know, are pretty large. A single braille dictionary is composed of fifteen to twenty volumes.

Braille was a great invention for the world's blind population, but not so great for its tree population.

"All right," I say.

"In the meantime, I've arranged for you to have a digital audiobook of our first short story, 'The Gift of the Magi.'"

"You paid for that out of your own pocket?"

She's silent, which I take for a yes.

"You really didn't have to do that, Mrs. Everbrook."

"Now, don't get all mushy on me, Will. I wasn't trying to be nice. I just didn't want you to have any excuses if you turned in your first paper late."

• • •

After English is biology, and then journalism. There's a restroom right outside Mrs. Everbrook's classroom that Mr. Johnston showed me yesterday, and I stop to use it. I slip into my desk about ten seconds after the bell rings. At the school for the blind, our teachers didn't mind if we arrived a little late. But that's not the case with Mrs. Everbrook.

She stops midsentence and addresses me. "Will, do you have a note for being late?"

"No," I say. "I was, uh, using the restroom."

"For today, I'll just give you a verbal warning. Next time, make it come out faster, or I will have to mark you as tardy."

Mrs. Everbrook returns to discussing story assignments.

"We've got two events that need a photographer this week. The first is the touring Vincent van Gogh exhibit that just came to PU."

PU is the unfortunate, but widely used, abbreviation for Plains University, the institution of higher learning that keeps the economy afloat in our little city. The marketing people at the school are always trying to "rebrand" it as PSU, as in PlainS University, but it never sticks. Everyone keeps calling it PU. It doesn't help that the school has an agriculture department that does something with fertilizer and stinks up the whole town a few times per semester.

"I know none of you probably give a hoot about art, but Toano's a pretty small place, and van Gogh's a pretty big deal, so I think it's worth covering. Cecily, you know more about art than the rest of your philistine classmates put together, so you'll be shooting that."

Cecily—the girl from yesterday. Who thought I was staring. The one I made cry.

"All right," says Cecily. "Thanks."

"We need a staff writer to accompany Cecily and cover the event. Volunteers?"

No one speaks. No volunteers. Why not? Then I wonder: *Is it because of me?* Is it because I stared at her yesterday and made her cry, and now everyone thinks she's weird? I start to feel sorry for her.

The seconds stretch like minutes, each sharp *tick... tick... tick* of the wall clock ringing painfully in my ears. I consider how she must feel.

She probably hates me for what I did to her, for embarrassing her like that. And I can't stand the thought of someone hating me. The art museum visit would be a chance to win her over, to prove that I'm a nice guy, a guy people like if they get to know me.

35

"I'll go," I say.

"Great, thanks, Will," says Mrs. Everbrook. "This will be for the news section."

A few minutes later, I hear someone approach and sit down at the desk beside me. I wait. Nothing happens. And then I feel a single finger brush the outside of my hand, requesting my attention.

"I'm sorry about yesterday," she says. "It's Cecily, by the way."

"I know. I know your voice," I mean. "Sorry. It won't happen again." I say.

"You mean because you're wearing sunglasses today?" she asks.

So she noticed. I absently push them up the bridge of my nose.

They feel clunky and awkward on my face. They are as tall as my thumb on the front and the sides, only tapering at the part that sit on my ears. It's like a megaphone calling attention to my blindness. But yesterday I realized that what Mom has always told me was correct: I should always wear my sunglasses. My eyes *do* make people uncomfortable. People like this girl Cecily.

"Yes, that's why I'm wearing them."

She shifts in her seat.

"If you want, I can drive us," she offers. "To the museum."

"You have a car?"

"My mom does. How about maybe we go tomorrow?"

"It's a date," I say, immediately cringing at my word choice.

As I head from journalism to lunch, I wonder if I will be able to sit with everyone from yesterday. I mean, if they decide they don't want the blind kid joining their table on an ongoing basis, it would be oh so easy for them to *just happen* to sit at a different one. I'd have no way of ever knowing where. Or why.

At the school for the blind, the loners moved silently, rarely giving away their voiceprint and remaining mostly unknown to all but their roommates. The opposite, having everyone recognize your voice, meant you were either notorious or popular. I happened to be popular.

At this school, though, I have no idea how many people have even noticed me so far. And if they have, it's probably only because I'm an anomaly.

I notice how much less obstructed my path is now that I'm walking alone, as opposed to when Mr. Johnston was guiding me through the hall yesterday and my cane was folded and hidden in my back pocket. Then I was merely a new student. Now I'm obviously a *blind* new student.

I walk to the same table as yesterday and set down my lunch bag.

"Hey, guys," I say, pretending I'm confident, that I'm not worried I might be speaking to an empty table.

"Yo," says Whitford.

"What's up?" says Ion.

"You're back!" says Nick.

They're still here, I think with a great sigh of relief.

"How's your second day of mainstreaming going?" asks Nick.

"I like how that can be a verb *or* an adjective," says Ion. "You *are mainstreaming* at a *mainstream* school."

"Or a noun," adds Whitford. "The *mainstream* school will funnel you into the *mainstream*."

"Exactly why this place sucks," says Nick. "Mainstream always equals suckitude."

There's a gap in the conversation, but I sense that it has continued in a wordless exchange of facial expressions. I read the braille label on a Tupperware container from my lunch bag. Carrots. Mom always packs carrots. I think she secretly believes my eyesight can be salvaged if I just consume enough beta-carotene.

Eventually Ion says, "So what do your parents do, Will?"

"My mom is a professional helicopter parent and country clubber. And my dad's a doctor."

"What kind of doctor?" asks Nick.

I was afraid he'd ask this. I try to avoid answering directly. I don't know Nick all that well yet, but I already know that if he finds out, he'll have a field day.

"Like, you know, sick people come to his place of business, and he makes them feel good," I say.

"A statement that could also describe a prostitute," says Nick. "I mean, what kind of medicine does he practice?"

I'm cornered. "He's a urologist," I admit.

"*No!*" says Nick in a tone of gleeful mock disbelief.

"Oh, grow up!" says Ion.

"A urologist? Like he—" says Nick.

"Yes," I say.

"So he's gay?" Nick asks.

"Seriously?" scolds Ion. "Just because you're a complete dick doesn't mean you have to be a homophobe."

I say, "He did create me with my mom, so I don't think—"

But Nick's on a roll now. "I don't get why any medical student would choose urology, you know? Like, why not plastic surgery? Now there's a job for you. Play with boobs all day and get paid big bucks for it."

"What are we? Schoolchildren?" says Ion.

But Nick's still going: "I just wonder about any straight male who says to himself, 'You know what I'd like to do for the rest of my life? Examine penises.'"

By way of changing the conversation, I tell them about the museum visit I have scheduled for tomorrow with the girl from journalism.

"What's her name?" asks Nick.

"Cecily."

"Wait. *Cecily Hoder?*" asks Whitford, surprised.

"Yeah."

No one says anything.

"What?" I ask.

"If she didn't have a different lunch period than us," Ion says, "Cecily Hoder would be sitting here. She's the fourth member of our academic quiz team."

CHAPTER 5

In the art museum the next afternoon, each click of my cane on the hard, smooth floor reverberates like a shotgun blast. It's so quiet I can hear a faint buzz overhead, presumably from the ceiling lights. That's a funny thing about artificial light: You can hear it. But I've never heard the sun, moon, or stars. Natural light, it seems, travels in silence. Like a Tesla.

Cecily and I stand in front of a painting, silent. No snaps of her camera yet. She's just looking at it, I guess.

Remembering that I'm here to make things up to her after our disastrous first encounter, I try to break the ice by asking her how she got into photography.

"Through painting, actually," she says.

"So why not..." I say. I speak carefully, lest I induce another tearful breakdown.

"Paint?" she suggests.

"Well, yeah."

"Oh, I can't paint."

"No?"

"Definitely not."

"I've never painted, but how hard can it be? You hold the brush and then you rub paint on the paper until it looks like what you see. Right?" I ask.

"Yeah, but it's not like that. You are *re-creating* the image. That takes talent."

"To paint what's right there in front of you?"

"Of course."

"I don't get it."

"Um, let me think of an example." She pauses. "Okay, it's like how you can be looking at something, a person or a beautiful landscape like, I don't know, the Grand Canyon, but then you take a photo with a cell phone camera and it doesn't look the same. It takes skill even to create photos that represent what the eye sees."

Sigh. Will people never learn? "Still doesn't mean much to me."

"Oh, right, sorry. I guess it's like . . . You know what my voice sounds like, right?"

"Yeah." I ponder her voice for a moment. It's controlled and pressurized, like the water flowing through a turbine in a dam. But dams don't just generate power. They are a barricade. They hold back a flood.

"And the sound of my voice is very clear coming through your ears?"

The question interrupts my thoughts about hydropower. "Sure."

42

"Can you imitate it?"

"How do you mean?"

"Like, can you re-create the sound of my voice using your own vocal cords?"

"Oh...I think I get it now."

"Right, and that's what's so cool about art," she says, speaking faster. "Van Gogh was an impressionist, so he wasn't even trying to paint scenes that look like what a person would see with their eyes. Sorry, is this weird to talk about? Like, seeing and stuff? I don't mean—"

"No, it's fascinating, actually. Please continue."

"All right, so a *realist* is an artist who paints an image that looks similar to what a good photographer could capture on film. That's, like, if you could imitate the sound of my speech with near-perfect accuracy using your own voice. But an *impressionist* paints not what the scene actually is, but what it *feels* like."

"It's distorted?"

"No, not distorted. It's...interpreted...represented in a different way. Like a metaphor. Like an impressionistic version of my voice might not sound like me at all, at least not in a literal sense. It might be a piece of music that when you hear it makes you think of my voice. You hear it and say, 'Yes, that captures the essence of what Cecily sounds like.'"

I'm silent.

"Sorry, did I lose you?" she asks. "I know I kind of geek out about—"

"No, I just—wow, that's a really good description.

Thank you. No one has ever explained art to me like that before."

"You're welcome," she says, more softly.

She removes the lens cap from her camera, and the shutter clicks a few times.

Trying to keep the conversation going, I ask, "So what sort of stuff did van Gogh paint?"

"Landscapes and plants, mostly."

"Not people?"

"He painted people, but that's not what he's known for."

"How come?"

She's silent for a moment. "Maybe because what is considered beautiful in nature has remained constant throughout history, but the definition of human beauty changes every few years based on how the media defines the so-called perfect body."

Just then a set of footsteps approaches and a voice interrupts us.

"Excuse me, sir, may I ask you a personal question?" he says.

"Yes, I'm blind," I say.

"Sorry, I didn't mean to be rude."

"What gave it away? Do my socks not match or something?"

"Well, no..." he stammers.

"I'm kidding. I've got a cane and sunglasses. Of course I'm blind."

"Listen," he says. "I'm a security guard. *The* security guard, actually. I travel with this exhibit. I just wanted to say that if you're interested, you are welcome to touch these paintings."

I'm stunned. It's not unusual these days for museums to allow the visually impaired to touch some artwork. But a van Gogh?

"For real?"

"Yes, sir. This is the personal collection of Edward Kramer. Mr. Kramer has a son with special needs, and he wants to be sure that people of all abilities can appreciate them. But you have to be really, really gentle. The paint is a century and a half old. Touch it as lightly as possible. And wash your hands first. Gets rid of the oil on your skin that can damage the paint."

"Fair enough. Where's the restroom?" I ask.

"I'll show you," says Cecily. "I want to make sure you go into the right one."

The guard walks away.

"Wait," I say, taken aback. "What was that supposed to mean?"

"Nothing."

"Were you making fun of blind people?"

"No, I would never—" She stops and sighs. "Yesterday, before journalism, you..."

"What?"

"You went into the girls' bathroom."

That hot feeling builds in my face. "Please tell me you're joking."

"I wish I was," she says.

"At least tell me you were the only one who saw."

"Uh…"

"How many more?"

"It's really not that big—"

"Two? Three?"

"Don't worry about—"

"Ten?"

"Twenty. Okay, more like twenty-five," she says. "Absolute max: thirty."

"THIRTY?"

"It was basically the whole journalism class, with the exception of Mrs. Everbrook. Everyone felt really terrible about it, if that's any consolation. And the doors are right beside each other, so you aren't even the first person to make the mistake."

"Well, you were the only one who told me," I say. "You took the hit. Thanks. That couldn't have been easy."

"The truth has a price," she says. "That's what my mom always says."

Her mom is right. It stings, knowing all those students were watching me make a fool of myself.

I go to the (correct) restroom and wash my hands. The first painting I touch is called *Les Alyscamps*.

"Let's play a game," I suggest. "I'll touch it and try to guess what it's a painting of."

"Okay," she says.

I start from the bottom, running my hands softly across the canvas the way I read braille. The paint has a dry, layered texture to it. There are places where the paint is globbed on smooth and thick, and others where it has tiny canyons of texture. I spread my fingers wider to absorb the shape of the bottom half of the canvas. The object in the painting starts out covering the entire width of the canvas, and then as it moves upward, it gets smaller and smaller until it ends in a point. I think of objects I know of with this shape.

"Is it a slice of pie?" I guess.

"Nope," she says.

"A piece of pizza?"

"Nope."

"A Dorito?"

"When was your last meal?"

I laugh. "But am I close?"

"No, it's not any kind of food. And for the record, I don't think Doritos had been invented yet."

"But it's triangle-shaped, right?"

She thinks for a moment. "Well...yeah, I guess it is," she says, as if she hadn't noticed this before.

"Fine, I give up. What is it?"

"A road."

"But roads are straight lines," I say, confused. "Is it an impressionistic street or something?"

"No, it's just the perspective."

I don't understand.

"You know," she adds when I say nothing. "Like, it gets smaller in the distance. Well, the street's not *actually* getting smaller—it's just how it looks when it's far away," she says.

"Yeah, I just don't understand what you're saying," I admit.

"Oh, I'm sorry," she says, a note of sensitivity entering her voice. "I just assumed... So I guess you don't know what perspective is?"

"I know what the word means," I say, sounding a little more defensive than I intended. "Like people have different perspectives on issues. Or people look at things from different perspectives. But how does that make the road a triangle?"

"Well, okay. Basically, as things get farther away, they look smaller," she explains patiently.

"They change size?"

"They don't actually change size. Just how much space they take up in your field of vision."

"Why?"

"Um, I don't really know, actually. It just is."

"So why is the street in the painting pointy?"

"Van Gogh is painting as if he's looking along the road, so the farther away it gets from him, the smaller it looks to him, until it disappears completely at the horizon."

"It just *disappears*?"

"Well, sure. You can't see forever."

"I know that the eyes can't see forever. But if I stand right beside this painting and touch the frame, and then step back to arm's length and touch it again, the frame feels like the same width in my hand. So this perspective thing...wow...that kind of blows my mind, Cecily."

"You're welcome, I guess?" she says, like a question. "I'm surprised you've never heard that before."

"Well, I mean, I moved away to the school for the blind when I was in kindergarten. I spent most summers at blind camps. So basically all my friends my whole life have been blind. Even many of the teachers at my school had visual impairments. So it was literally—"

"The blind leading the blind," she interrupts.

I touch a few of the other paintings, and she explains each one to me. Listening to descriptions of art in this way lights up distant, rarely used corners of my brain.

"There's another room," she says. "Do you want me to, um, lead you there? Like with your arm?"

"Guide. We call it guiding. And yes, please."

"So how does it work?"

"Just reach your elbow a little toward me, and I'll hold it."

When I grab her arm, I feel this tingle, almost like touching something that has an electric current running through it. It's not painful. Just sort of shocking. I jerk my hand away.

"I'm sorry," she says, her voice shrinking. "Did I do it wrong?"

"No, that was fine. I just... Never mind. You did great."

I reach for her arm a second time, and when I touch her sweater, I feel that charge again.

Cecily guides me into the other room.

"You know how many paintings van Gogh created?" she asks.

"No idea."

"Almost a thousand."

"Wow."

"And you know how many he sold?"

"All of them, I guess. I mean, he was a really famous painter, right?"

"Not till long after he died. In his entire life, he sold only one of his paintings."

"One?" I ask in disbelief.

"One."

"That's why I relate to him, I think," she says thoughtfully. "He was born at the wrong time."

"So you're like some kind of unrecognized genius, too?" I realize I'm still holding her arm, so I squeeze it playfully.

She laughs, and it works its way into my brain, reminding me of what she said earlier. Her laughter is like impressionist art. Because it captures the essence of itself, the essence of laughter.

"No, just born at the wrong time in history."

"A lot of blind people feel that way, too," I say. "Hundreds of years ago, most people were doing manual labor, like working farms or pulling plows or whatever. You didn't need extremely clear vision for stuff like that. You could go a lifetime without realizing you couldn't see as well as everyone else."

"But now we are in the information age," she fills in.

"Exactly. Which started with the printing press, and now our society is based on communicating by words and pictures. It's called 'the tyranny of the visual.' Sorry, I didn't mean to regurgitate everything from my seventh-grade History of Visual Impairment class."

"No, not at all," she says, and sounds like she means it.

"Although in the last couple years, technology *has* been making things a lot easier," I add.

She guides me up to a painting, and we stop. Normally at this point, I would let go of a guide's arm. But I don't. Instead, I loop my hand through the wrist strap on my cane so I can touch the painting with that hand while my other one stays connected to Cecily.

And then I catch myself. Why am I still holding on to this girl's arm? I've already reached point B.

So I let go as I examine the painting with my other hand.

Cecily describes the painting to me in between snaps of her camera. One of van Gogh's many self-portraits, she explains. He looks gaunt and soulful. She says there are hints in his eyes of the depression that will eventually claim his life, when he committed suicide at age thirty-seven.

"It has a lot of oranges and reds in it," she says. "But I guess you don't know what those look like, huh?"

"Not so much."

"Those are considered warm colors. So they're like the heat of the sun or the smell of the fall."

"Sorry," I say. "That's poetic, but it doesn't help me."

"Can you not even...like, imagine a color?" she asks.

I hear more visitors shuffle into the room, voices soft as they comment on the artwork.

"Even if I could, how would I know I'm imagining a color when I've never seen one before?" I ask. "It's, like, how do you know that when you see red, it's the same red as everyone else sees? Maybe what they call red looks to them like what you call blue? There's no way of knowing if your experience of a certain color is the same."

"But I can close my eyes and see a color in my mind. Can you not do that?"

I chuckle.

"What?" she asks.

"Let me put it this way: Try to imagine a color you've never seen before. Like, a brand-new color that was just invented and has never before existed. What would it look like?"

She is silent.

"Well?" I ask.

"You're right," she says. "It's impossible."

"That's how it is for me. Except with all colors. And all two-dimensional shapes. And everything you see in these paintings. You have to understand that my mind developed differently because, unlike most blind people, I have never seen anything with my eyes."

"You were completely blind from birth?"

"Right," I say.

"So you're trying to tell me you belong to a pretty exclusive club?" she says playfully.

"I'd show you the membership card, but you wouldn't be able to read it. It's written in braille."

She laughs, but then says seriously, "I'm sorry."

"For what?"

"That you have to live that way. It must be so frustrating."

If there's one thing I don't like, it's people feeling sorry for me.

"What do you mean?" I say, trying to limit the irritability creeping into my voice. "You think my experience of the world is less rich because I'm blind?"

"Well, you're missing out on so many—"

"That's sightist, Cecily. Assuming that blind people can't have a full life because they don't have eyesight. My sensory experience isn't *less* than yours. It's just different."

"I'm so sorry. I didn't mean—"

"Why don't you take your pictures so we can get out of here? I'll go interview the guard to get some quotes for my article."

"Want me to guide you back to him?"

"No, I remember the route."

CHAPTER 6

After I get home from the museum, I go to my bedroom and plop down on the bed to listen to music. It's the bedroom I grew up in before I went to the school for the blind. Other kids, I guess, have posters on their walls with photos of stuff they like to look at. Cecily's probably has paintings. No, forget Cecily. She was rude to me. I don't care what her room looks like.

When I was a kid, Mom helped me decorate my bedroom walls with scratch-and-sniff stickers. Each wall has its own category. The wall with my closet is sweet food (fruit, desserts, and the like), the wall with my desk is savory food, and the one by my bed is scents of nature.

In total, I have 187 different fragrances on the walls of my room. When I was a kid, I wished I had that many fingers so I could scratch them simultaneously and find out what all the scents in the world smelled like together. (As it turns out, I'm able to experience this by simply walking into Toano High School's cafeteria.)

My bedspread is covered in wispy threads like the fur

of a freakishly fluffy pet. Lying on my back, I rub the pine-scented sticker on the wall and inhale through my nose. I moved away soon after we put the stickers up, so they've just been chilling here for ten years, waiting for their fragrance to be scratched open. The softness of the bed and the whiff of the sticker, however, keep getting interrupted by the echo of Cecily's laugh. I keep thinking about how much I liked being with her at that gallery. Which is annoying, because I'm still mad about what she said. I claw at a grass-scented sticker in an attempt to drown her out with olfactory overload.

Seeking a different distraction, I open my laptop to write my article about the van Gogh exhibit. I don't include anything about what it felt like to touch Cecily's arm or how it felt to be insulted by her at the end, of course, because that's not anyone's business, but I do write about how the owner has a special-needs child, which meant I was allowed to touch the paintings. I describe the feel of the crackled paint under my fingertips. As for the museum itself, I note the way our footsteps reverberated through the museum's reverent silence as we walked through its heavily air-conditioned and dehumidified climate.

The garage-door opener downstairs cranks to life. Mom and Dad must be back from their errands. I used to hear the car engine before the garage opened. Now it just starts to lift with no warning. Stupid Tesla.

A minute later, I hear Mom climbing the stairs and then there's a knock at my door.

"Will, come down to the family room!" she says. "We have a surprise for you!"

"I'm doing homework."

"Just finish it later."

This is quite possibly the first time my mother has ever encouraged me to procrastinate on my homework. (Even at boarding school, the long arm of the mom-law followed my studies and grades with the utmost care.) So I leave my laptop and walk downstairs.

In a voice more appropriate for giving a speech to hundreds, she announces, "Your father and I wanted to be able to start going on family bike rides. So after your dad got home from the operating room today, we purchased a tandem bike for you and me to share!"

Great. Just what I've always wanted.

We go out to the garage, where I find Dad has been checking the tire pressure and lubricating the gears on the bike.

"Guys, I've never even ridden a bike before," I say.

"It's all right," says Dad. "As the front rider, your mother can keep you balanced as long as you maintain speed."

"If you say so," I mutter.

"You have to pedal at the same time," instructs Dad. "Sydney, warn Will before you turn or brake so he is prepared. Be careful."

We push off, and Dad gets on his bike to follow us.

"Stop sign," warns Mom. I feel the bike decelerate. Before we tip over, she puts a foot down on the pavement to steady us.

We've gone only one block, and I already officially hate Dad's beloved sport of cycling. I mean, yeah, the breeze feels kind of nice, but I can replicate that sensation by putting my face in front of a house fan. Riding on a tandem bike mostly makes me feel like a prisoner. The rider in the back has no brakes, no steering, no choice.

We ride mostly in silence for a few minutes, aside from Mom's occasional outbursts ("Isn't this great!").

Then she says, "I have something else exciting to discuss."

Because of course she does. There had to be a *reason* to trap me on this bike other than the ride itself.

She continues, "There's an experimental operation being tested at your dad's hospital. It has to do with retinal stem cell transplants. If you are accepted as a candidate, it could give you eyesight! Full eyesight! Can you imagine?"

Unwittingly, my pulse quickens. "Dad, is this true?"

His tone is far more sober. "It's not even a stage-one clinical trial yet. Still completely experimental. Honestly, there's a very small chance of success."

"But if it did work, I mean—it could give me eyesight?"

"I would wait for them to test the procedure on other patients first. There are so many risks associated with an operation. People don't even realize—every time a surgeon opens an incision, you are subjecting yourself to risk of infection, physician error, complications—"

"But just think, Will," counters Mom. "If it *was* successful, you could have twenty-twenty vision. Isn't that worth at least considering? Just go in for an initial consultation. I've already made the appointment for you next Thursday."

Hold up. She already made the appointment?

I'm tempted to say no just out of principle. I'm sixteen years old. She can't go around making appointments for me without asking me first.

But on the other hand, what if it worked? What if I could . . . see?

"I guess it can't hurt to talk to them," I say. "I'll go to the consultation. But under one condition."

"What?" asks Mom.

"I go by myself. This is my decision, and I don't want you or anyone else making it for me."

"Well, sweetie, of course it's your decision, but you'll need me in the room—"

"No," I say. "Not even in the building. You drop me off, I go in by myself. That's the deal. Take it or leave it."

"Fine," says Mom. "But I'll wait in the parking lot so you can text if you need me."

• • •

That evening, I'm sitting on my bed listening to the recording of "The Gift of the Magi." It's actually really short, and after it's finished I listen to some blog posts on my phone about how the invention of the iPod led to a boom in the audiobook industry when Siri interrupts to say, "Notification: Message from Cecily." I tap my phone and listen to the text.

"Hi."

I tap once more and Siri reads it again.

"Hi."

Really? That's it?

"Hi."

Just one word: *Hi*. What does that mean? Does she want to apologize? Is she trying to initiate conversation but doesn't know what to say? Does she pity poor blind Will and feel obligated to send condolences via text?

How do I respond to such a vague opening statement? I run through a variety of options in my mind. I scratch a sticker and soak up its aroma of campfire. Finally I settle on a proportionate response.

"Hi," I reply.

Her next text comes back almost immediately.

Cecily: I feel really stupid.

Me: Why?

Cecily: About what I said at the end.

Me: It's OK.

Cecily: No, it's not. I was wrong.

Me: Thanks for saying that. Consider yourself forgiven.

I migrate from my bed to my desk. The wall of the savory. I scratch the pizza sticker and take a big whiff. I scratch a hot dog sticker and find it blends surprisingly well with the waning aroma of pizza.

Then she writes back.

Cecily: That's really nice to hear.

Me: I'm a pretty nice guy...when I'm not accidentally staring at people.

Cecily: Can you do emoji?

Me: I don't know. How do you do it?

Cecily: They're little pictures you send by text. Here I'll send you one and you can tell me what your phone says.

On her next message, my phone reads, "Smiling face, dancing monkey, cat face with wry smile."

I text her what it said.

"Cool," she replies. "So it's reading you the names of the pictures. What does this one say?"

I listen to her next message and tell her what it said: "Smiling pile of poop."

I wonder what that could possibly look like. And, for that matter, why would anyone ever send it?

Then she sends me three more. Siri reads me the message: "Small up-pointing triangle, large red down-pointing triangle, black left-pointing double triangle."

I write: "?"

There's a pause before Cecily replies with a long text: "Before today, I never noticed how roads look like triangles as they disappear into the horizon. I only saw roads getting smaller as they got farther away. Now, thanks to you, I'm seeing triangles everywhere."

I smile. I open Facebook and send her a friend request.

There's a knock on my door. My door, by the way, is covered on both sides with scratch-and-sniff stickers that fall more into the "odor" category than "scent." Rotten eggs, gasoline, smelly socks, skunks. That kind of thing. Sort of an olfactory-based KEEP OUT sign.

"William, time for dinner," says Dad.

"Okay, just a sec."

I text Cecily, "Gotta go, family dinner."

I get one more text from her before I head downstairs to dinner. "Just accepted your request. Glad we are officially friends now."

CHAPTER 7

That Friday I sit alone at lunch. The academic quiz team is at an away tournament all day. So Cecily's not in journalism, either.

But after school, Ion texts me to say that they won, so they're going out for a celebratory dinner and would I like to join them?

I've never been to the restaurant before, so after Mom drops me off—I decline her offer to park and guide me in—I stand outside and hope someone from the group will arrive to show me inside.

A door swings open, dinging a bell. I recognize the next sound: the deliberate but controlled steps, treading gently, as if she's trying not to leave footprints. I've never seen a footprint, of course, but my understanding is that the harder you press, the more of an impression you leave behind.

"Hi, Will, it's Cecily."

"I know," I say.

"I was waiting inside and saw you standing here, so..."

Her voice drifts off as she guides me inside, and we wait in the front of the restaurant, me still holding her arm.

Then I get a text from Ion. She's so sorry, but Whitford is sick and she is going to have to skip the dinner so she can take care of him.

"That's weird," says Cecily.

"What?"

"He didn't seem sick at the tournament today."

Then Cecily's phone buzzes. It's a text from Nick. His mom is going out, and he has to babysit his brother.

Well, this is awkward. No longer is it a celebration dinner with five people. Now it's like...a date.

And I mean, Cecily is a nice person and all, but dating is the last thing on my mind at the moment. I've had girlfriends before, and it was cool and everything, but it brings all kinds of drama. And I've got plenty of drama to deal with already, thank you very much.

As if she were reading my mind, Cecily asks, "Do you want a ride home?"

But I realize, if I go home, Mom will think my new friends stood me up. Cue the hints about returning to the school for the blind. So leaving early is far worse than a possibly awkward dinner with the photographer girl from journalism class.

"How about we just stay for dinner?"

"You sure?" she asks. "I mean, it'll just be...you know, me."

"Yeah, definitely," I say. "We're already here. Might as well eat."

She guides me in a pattern of ninety-degree turns, left, right, left, right, around the tables in the diner. We end at a countertop bar with tall stools covered in smooth plastic. Across the counter, a mere arm's length away, I hear the sizzle of meat on a grill and the hiss of boiling oil in a fryer.

I hear Cecily pop the lens off her camera and snap a few photos. There's a whisper of plastic twisting over plastic as she adjusts the lens—zooming or focusing or something—and takes a few more.

I ask, "For Instagram? Hashtag food porn?"

She laughs a little.

"You're on Instagram?" she asks, surprised.

"Yeah. I like the captions. Anyway, what's your picture of?"

"Us," she says simply.

"You and me?"

"Well, mostly you. The camera is covering my face. There's a mirror across from us."

"What I would give to have a mirror," I say. "I'm constantly wondering if my shirt is on backward or if my hair is sticking up or something."

"You're not missing out. Mirrors just make people overly concerned about their appearance," she says dismissively.

"Really? I've always assumed that if I could see myself

in a mirror, I would be less concerned about my appearance. Because I wouldn't have to wonder what I looked like anymore. I could stop worrying about it."

"In my experience, it's usually the other way around."

"Is that a mirror joke?"

"What?"

"*The other way around.* Because isn't everything flipped in mirrors? Like upside down?"

"Close. Wrong axis. Everything is flipped left to right. It's backward, not upside down. But no, that wasn't a joke. I mean, I think it works the opposite of what you're saying: Mirrors make everyone *more* worried about their appearance."

I hear the swish of a waitress walking by on the other side of the counter. (And yes, I infer her gender based on the sound of her footsteps, an educated guess I'm usually right about.)

I want to get the waitress's attention to ask for menus. It's silly, but part of me hopes this will impress Cecily—that she will notice how sensitive my hearing is, or at least that she'll feel like she's hanging out with a normal person who knows when a waitress is walking by, not a helpless blind kid who needs someone else to flag down a server for him.

"Excuse me, can we get some menus?" I ask.

"What are you, blind?" the waitress snaps.

I squirm. Her tone implies that she was using that word *blind* to mean my question was stupid.

She wouldn't be the first, unfortunately. One time, for a paper at my old school, I searched *blind* in the thesaurus app on my phone. The synonyms included *ignorant, oblivious, irrational, mindless, reckless,* and *violent.* Kind of rude if you are actually, you know, blind. But her accusation also happens to be factual enough to stand up in a court of law: I am 100 percent legally blind.

"Yes, actually, I am blind."

"Oh my *God,* I am *so* sorry!" she says, realizing. "Holy...oh, wow...I am the worst person ever. I am so sorry. *God.* That was so rude. I'm just having the worst day—not that that's any excuse—I just wasn't thinking."

"It happens," I say.

"The menu is already on the counter. I'm sorry we don't have it in braille or anything. Do you want me to, like, read it to you?"

"I'll read it for him," Cecily says coolly.

Cecily talks me through the menu. A few minutes later, the waitress returns for our orders.

"I'm not really hungry," says Cecily. "I'll just have a Diet Coke, please."

"And what will he be having?" the waitress asks Cecily.

"*I* will be having the grilled cheese," I say.

"Oh, get it cut into triangles instead of rectangles," suggests Cecily. "It tastes so much better that way."

"Really?"

"Really."

"Please prepare the sandwich as the lady suggests."

"One grilled cheese, sliced into triangles," repeats the waitress, making audible scratches with a pen.

After the waitress walks away, Cecily asks, "So how come you signed up for journalism class?"

"I want to be a writer. Seemed like good practice. You?"

"Same. Except I want to be a photographer."

"Of nature, I assume?"

"Yeah. I want to see the world through the lens of my camera. That's everything to me, everything I want."

"No house with a white picket fence and two-point-four babies?"

"Well...it's not like I don't want those things. It's just that I've always assumed..." She trails off.

"What?"

"That I will never be in a relationship," she says. And then she adds quickly, "If I was, you know, traveling that much."

A few seconds later, the grilled cheese arrives. Cecily is right. It does taste better this way.

"Are you going to audition for the morning announcements show?" I ask, mouth still partially full of grilled cheese.

"On the school TVs?" she asks. "Definitely not."

"Not your thing?"

"No. I mean, there's a vote. You know that, right?

The school elects the next semester's hosts based on the audition."

"So?"

"I just don't think I could ever win a vote like that."

"How come?"

"Weren't there popular kids at the school for the blind?"

"Sure, there were." In fact, I was one of them. But I don't tell her that. "That doesn't matter, though. I think you have . . . well, a really nice voice. I would vote for you."

"Why don't *you* audition?" she says.

"Me?"

"Yeah, why not?"

"I can't read printed text. I mean, I assume they are reading scripts or something, right?"

"Oh," she says, her voice dropping. "You're right. They read off teleprompters that scroll the words in front of the camera."

"So yeah, there's that. I mean, it would be cool and all, but I just don't think it would work."

"But what if—what if we could find a way to *make* it work?"

"Like what?"

"Like, I don't know. I could read the announcements into a little microphone that would play them into an earpiece you were wearing. Something like that?"

"No way," I say, imagining all the ways that could go wrong. "It would never work."

"Whitford is pretty good with tech stuff. Maybe he can figure out a way that you could read the script yourself."

I'm not sure how this conversation got so turned around. The point was that I thought *Cecily* should try out. *She's* the one with the beautiful voice.

"Fine," I say. "I'll make you a deal."

"What?"

"I'll try out if you will."

"But I'm really not—"

"That's my offer," I say.

She hesitates for a while.

"Fine. We'll both audition."

"If we figure out a way to make it work for me."

"We'll find a way. Don't worry. I'll help you."

CHAPTER 8

Dr. Bianchi, the doctor who is doing the experimental surgery, works in an office building at PU's med school. True to our agreement, Mom drops me off at the curb after school on Thursday.

"There's a revolving door," she warns. "You sure you don't want me to guide you in?"

"I'm sure."

"How will I know you made it safely to your appointment?"

"I'll text you when I'm there, okay?"

"If I don't hear anything within ten minutes, I'm going to come inside and find you."

"Fine."

I try to walk at a normal pace from the car to the building; I don't want Mom to see me hurrying to beat her ten-minute deadline. Once I've navigated the revolving door, however, I hustle across the lobby to the elevator.

Because of the way the braille numbers are staggered

on the inside of two columns of buttons, it's not entirely clear which button corresponds to the twelfth floor.

I press one, and the elevator goes up. When it stops and the doors open, I walk across the hall, only to discover that the first door I come to is 602. I'm looking for office 1239.

I quickly review my training with Mrs. Chin, hoping I can fix this problem before Mom helicopters in, no doubt with a full SWAT team in tow to rescue me.

If the braille was lined up better, I could use a basic blind ninja trick: hold my hand on the button I pressed and wait till the doors open and then start to close, then press it again to see if they reopen.

Of course, it's possible that I pressed the wrong button in the first place. It's also possible someone on the sixth floor pressed the Up button, but when my elevator stopped for him and he saw a blind guy standing in it, the guy froze, not wanting to infringe on my space, but also not wanting to make noise, lest I detect his presence and think him blind-phobic.

I get back on the elevator and press the Lobby button, which is helpfully embossed with a five-pointed star. From there I press every single button and count the number of times the doors open. I am painfully aware of how each wasted floor is another few seconds closer to Mom's humiliating arrival, but it's the only way to be sure I'm on number twelve.

I find the office, and a receptionist ushers me into an examination room. I sit and wait on a soft bench covered with crinkly paper. I check my phone. Good news: That elevator ordeal took only five minutes. Bad news: I get no service in here and can't text Mom. So to prevent her from bursting in at some point and making me look like a child in front of my new doctor, I have to make the only slightly less childlike request of using the receptionist's phone to call her and say I made it to the office safely.

"Hello, Will," says Dr. Bianchi when he enters the examination room, bringing with him a whiff of cigarette smoke. "Or do you prefer William?"

"Will is fine."

"Nice to meet you. You want to touch my face?"

He has an accent. *You wanta to toucha my face-ah?*

"I'm just kidding," he adds. "That is a little of the blind humor for you, yes?"

I chuckle. "Good one."

"You like music, Will?"

"Music? It's okay."

"I love music. I shall turn it on for us. You like the opera?"

"Sure."

"Here is another thing all the people believe about visual impairment," he says. "You all love to touch the faces, and you are all musical geniuses? Yes?"

"Yeah, people are always surprised that I want to be a writer instead of a musician."

"You wish to be a writer?"

"Yes."

"Very good."

He presses a button, and opera music turns on. He turns down the volume so it's just a background.

"There we go," he says. "One thing that is true, though—those who were born blind have a more developed sense of touch and hearing. For how long have you lacked eyesight, Will?"

"I was born without vision."

"In my office, Will, we always say *eyesight*, not *vision*," he explains. "Because they are not the same, yes?"

"I guess not," I concede.

"Eyesight is in the eyes. Vision is more. It is in the mind. The heart. The soul. But I digress. Let me ask you. Why do you want eyesight?"

"Why not?" I say, as if the question is pretty self-explanatory.

"Yes, why not? But again. This is the important question." He emphasizes those two words: *important question*. "Why do you want eyesight?"

"I think it would make my life better. Like, you know, reading and stuff. Have you heard of the 'tyranny of the visual'?"

"Yes, of course. Since so many of us in today's world rely on sight because of the mass media, living in our society is now more difficult for the blind."

"Right. So I think having vision—that is, *eyesight*—would improve my life."

He pauses and then says, "Will, do you know why I came to this country?"

"No."

"I have lived here for twenty years. I moved to America from Italy because PU has one of the best medical research programs in my field in the entire world. So I want to live here for a better career so I can give the better life for my family. So I understand this. When you say you want the better life, I understand this."

I don't say anything. The opera singer's voice shakes with vibrato.

"And I am one of the few surgeons who practice this surgery because I think it can offer a better life. Another reason humans have evolved to rely on eyesight as the primary sense is because it has the best spatial resolution."

"Sorry," I say. "I don't think I know what that is."

"Say you are in a restaurant, listening to another table. Easy enough to accomplish. But if you try to listen to two different conversations at different tables simultaneously, you find the limitation of hearing. You can't concentrate on both at once. But a person with eyesight can see and process hundreds of objects and colors at the same time. This is spatial resolution."

He pauses and then says, as if closing his argument, "So this is why I think eyesight can give you the better life."

I ask, "Can you help me see, Dr. Bianchi?"

He thinks for a moment. "It is a possibility," he concludes, in a tone that suggests I've cleared his first hurdle. "But several things stand in our way."

"Like what?"

"First, we must get the B-scan. To see if your congenital blindness makes you a candidate for the stem cell operation."

"Okay. A B-scan. Then what?"

"Then we must find a stem cell donor."

"If we do, that's it? Then I can see?"

"If only, Will, if only. No, then we must give your eyes a month to heal. After this, then we look for a cornea-transplant donor."

"So there are two surgeries?" I ask.

"Yes. First you need retinal stem cells. After that, we wait one month for you to heal. Then we have a two-week window. During that time, you can get corneas."

"So we need to find a donor? Um, how about one of my parents?"

He chuckles. "No, you cannot ask someone to do this for you. Not a living person. You need an organ donor, a cadaver who is recently deceased due to traumatic accident. But with the eyes intact. And for this donor we can only wait."

"What if we don't find a donor within the two weeks?"

"Donors are relatively easy to find. Sadly, accidents happen every day. And rarely are the eyes damaged."

"But if it did happen? If two weeks passed without us finding a donor?"

"If we miss the window, this is not a surgery we can do for another time. You would be staying blind forever."

Yikes.

I'm not sure how to take this. "Okay, let's assume we

find a donor, and I have the operation. Then I can see? Is that it?"

He chuckles again. "Oh, no, Will, that is only the beginning. After the operation, this is when the real work must begin."

"What do you mean?"

"Because you have never had eyesight, your visual cortex, the region of the brain that processes sight, has developed differently. If the visual cortex is stimulated with magnetic waves, the person with eyesight sees a flash of light. But for the person born blind, when the visual cortex is stimulated with the magnetic waves, he feels a tingling on his tongue or his fingers. Do you understand why?"

"No," I admit.

"The brain rewires itself to solve the problems it is given. This is called neuroplasticity. In a blind person, who does not need the visual cortex for processing eyesight, the visual cortex will instead be used to process taste or touch."

"Is that reversible?" I ask. "Would I be able to use that part of my brain for eyesight?"

"This is what we hope. I would provide you therapy and monitor your progress, but mostly it would just take time. You would be like, if I may say so, a newborn baby. After the surgery. You would have to *learn* how to see."

"But I *could* learn? With practice?"

"Hopefully. There are a number of risks. You may also lapse into confusion for some time, or for all time."

That catches me off guard. "I'm sorry. Did you say 'for all time'?"

"It is a possibility," he says reluctantly.

"Like, for the rest of my life? You mean I might go crazy?"

"The operation is full of risks, Will. It is a decision you must make for yourself."

I've had fantasies about eyesight. Like, if I could just magically have eyesight given to me or whatever. Of course I have. I think about it sometimes. And I've always just thought that it would all happen instantly. I'd open my eyelids and—poof—the world would open up to me.

Dr. Bianchi just crushed that dream.

"So can I think about it for a while?" I ask.

"I insist that you do. Think as long as you need. And discuss it with your family. But as long as you're here, would you like to get a preliminary B-scan to see if you are a candidate?"

"Sure, but can I, um, use your phone?" I ask. "I need to, um, call my mom and tell her I'm going to be a bit longer."

"Of course," he says.

• • •

On the drive home, I get a text from Whitford inviting me to "Settlers Sunday" this weekend. The entire quiz team will be there, he says.

There are many board games made specifically for blind

people. We have a few downstairs, in fact. I'm not going to bring one of those over and force everyone to play, but I do want to make friends. I want to fit in at this school. And Whitford lives just around the corner anyway. So I agree to go. I'll be "playing" Settlers, even though I won't really be able to participate at all. Hey, maybe one of them can move my piece for me. Yeah, that plan always works out *great*.

It makes me wonder, though. What if I could one day play board games without help? What if I could use my eyes to see where my own piece on the board should go?

The truth is, I've always wanted eyesight. I mean, obviously. I'd love to be able to see. It's not like I'm unhappy with myself the way I am or bitter about being blind or anything. I get along all right. I'm fine with who I am.

But if there's a chance I could gain eyesight, I mean, come on. Plenty of people go from sighted to blind. But how many people can say they've gone from blind to sighted? And how many details does most of the world take for granted, colors and shapes that I would be able to notice and appreciate? Normally, you learn to see for the first time as a baby and don't remember it. But getting eyesight for the first time as a teenager, when you can observe and remember every moment of the experience, that's much more than a once-in-a-lifetime opportunity. It would be like winning the lottery. I could live a thousand lifetimes or a million lifetimes and not get the chance to try something as cool as that again.

CHAPTER 9

On Sunday, it takes a while to persuade Mom to let me walk to Whitford's by myself. It's literally only three houses away. Perhaps, I think, living independently is something of a lofty goal, after all. Not because it is so terribly difficult for me to get by on my own, but because my mother simply won't let me.

I leave the house and walk left down the sidewalk. My mind keeps rewinding to the appointment with Dr. Bianchi. Would I really want to try the operation? Will I even qualify as a candidate? I count two driveways and then turn left at the intersection. Whitford's house, Siri tells me, is now on my left.

But at the end of the driveway, I stop. Do I seriously want to go to a *board game party*? I won't be able to play the game. Which will be awkward. Probably even more so for everyone else than for me.

This was stupid. I am going to walk back home.

"You just going to stand there all night?" a voice says

from about ten feet away. "Or are you going to come inside?"

I jump. "Jeez! You scared me!"

Cecily laughs.

I ask, "How long have you been standing there?"

"The whole time you have. I saw you coming and thought I would wait for you to come inside with me, but, uh, you never did. Were you waiting for someone who could guide you in or something?"

"Actually—yeah, that's what I was doing, I guess."

I don't tell her that I could have navigated to the front door without a guide. There's almost always a sidewalk through the front yard that leads directly to the entrance of a house. Or at least, that's what Mrs. Chin taught us.

"Come on, let's go in," she says, offering her arm.

At the front door, I meet Whitford's parents, both professors at PU.

"Nice to meet you, Dr. Washington and Dr. Washington," I say.

"You can call us *Mr.* and *Mrs.* Washington," says Whitford's dad. "We're not so pretentious as to require the use of honorifics in our home."

He and Mrs. Whitford burst into peals of laughter. Cecily and I chuckle politely.

They show us to the kitchen table.

"Hey, Nick, Ion, Whitford!" says Cecily. At first I think naming each person at the table is an odd greeting.

Then I realize it was for my benefit, to tell me who is in the room.

"Cecily, I see you've brought us a new Settler of Catan!" says Nick in an affected English-narrator voice.

Cecily replies in kind. "Indeed I have, good sir."

As I sit down in a wooden chair beside Cecily, I hear the rattle of game pieces inside a cardboard box.

I shouldn't be here. What a disaster waiting to happen. If only I'd gone back home before Cecily saw me outside!

As if she somehow knows how I'm feeling, Cecily grabs my hand and gives it a quick squeeze.

"Will and I will be on a team together," she says.

I tense up. I'm torn between my bad memories of the last time I relied on another player and the cold hard truth that I can't actually play at all if I don't have help.

"Good, because I don't have the expansion pack," says Whitford. "We can only have four players."

Well, then. My hand has been forced. I guess I'm on a team.

Whitford says, "Cecily and Will, you guys want some snacks? I've got cookies, Doritos, Skittles—"

"Sweet! Skittles, definitely," I say.

Whitford pours some Skittles into a bowl and sets it in front of me. I eat them one at a time, smelling each candy first to guess the flavor before I put it in my mouth. I'm usually right. Skittles are my favorite. Always have been, since I was little.

"It's my week to set up the map, right?" asks Ion.

"Indeed," says Nick.

"In that case, I'll take the terrain hexes and harbor pieces, please."

"You got it," says Nick.

"I'll teach you to play as we go along," Cecily says softly to me.

"If I ever invent a board game," Nick says, shuffling through the box, "I'll make sure the title starts with the same first letter as a day of the week. I think that's the key to success: an alliterative title so people naturally have a weekly standing game night."

"That's probably why Settlers has blown up," says Ion. "They've got the whole weekend on lockdown. Settlers Sunday *or* Settlers Saturday."

"Ditto for Scrabble, Snakes and Ladders, and Sorry," says Whitford.

Nick adds, "It continues with Monopoly Monday, Trivial Pursuit Tuesday, et cetera."

"What about checkers?" asks Whitford. "Isn't that the most popular board game of all time?"

"So glad you brought that up," says Nick. "Checkers was actually invented in ancient Egypt to amuse King Ramses, the pharaoh. Homer references the game in his writings, as does Plato. But for most of history, checkers has been referred to as 'draughts,' and while I can't attest to all languages where the game has flourished, in English we can see that following our alliterative formula, every single day can be named a Draught Day. Thus it can be played daily, explaining its position as the king of all board games."

There's a stunned silence after Nick finishes his speech.

"Drops microphone, walks away," says Ion.

"How do you *know* stuff like that?" asks Whitford.

"I'm on the quiz team, bitches," says Nick.

"So am I...but seriously...*the entire history of checkers?*" says Whitford.

"Okay, fine. I just read about it the other day," admits Nick. "I basically brought up that whole thing about the board games on certain days hoping someone would ask about checkers. But you have to admit...it sounded impressive."

"If you're done showing off now, I'll take the number tokens and robber, please," says Ion.

Nick's fingers return to rummaging the box for the requested items.

"So, are you guys going to homecoming?" I ask, trying to sound casual.

"Stand around with a bunch of awkward adolescents trying to dance while listening to sellout pop music under the Orwellian eyes of a hundred chaperones? Count me out," says Nick.

"Whitford and I are going," says Ion. "Cecily, are you?"

"I don't think it's really my scene," says Cecily.

The game begins, and Cecily narrates what's happening and explains each decision we have to make in our turns. The game has something to do with a map. The object is to build roads and establish settlements in order to accumulate something called victory points. Cecily consults with me about whether to build a road or a settlement depending on the resource cards we have. I touch the little rod piece that represents a road and the house-shaped one that represents a settlement. Apparently settlements can be turned into cities, which are represented by the most complex-feeling piece of all.

Cecily takes a bunch of photos while we play. She's testing a macro lens she just got off Craigslist. The lens, she explains, is designed to focus up close on tiny objects like game pieces. Gathering around the screen on her camera, the others agree that it does create a cool effect as Cecily tries to describe it to me.

Ion ends up winning the game, but if there were victory points for trash talking, Nick would have had it in the bag.

As my friends slide the game pieces across the table and drop them back into the box, I mention the meeting with Dr. Bianchi.

The packing of the game comes to an abrupt halt. The group is riveted.

"That's way cool," says Nick.

"Is it something you want?" asks Cecily.

"I have to get the test results to see if I qualify. That's step one. Then, I don't know. We'll see."

There's a pause, and Whitford says, "Well, I've rigged up a new reading device for you, but maybe you won't need it for much longer after all."

"Need what?" I ask.

"Cecily told me you wanted to try out to host the morning announcements."

I didn't so much *want* to as agreed to if she would do it, too.

"I might have figured out a way to make it work."

"You have?"

"Ever heard of a 'refreshable braille display'? It's pretty cool. I mean, I'm a gadget guy. I just love stuff like this. But it's this flat tablet that has a bunch of tiny rods in it that pop up to form braille letters in real time. When you finish reading a line of the braille, the rods reassemble to create the surface for the next line of text."

"Wow, that's so cool," says Ion.

"I know, right?" says Whitford. "I found a way to make it all work together. I found an app that allows a tele-prompter on this iPad"—I hear him tap the device—"to be controlled by an iPhone. So another host could control the script on the teleprompter by scrolling on the iPad with her finger off-camera, which controls the text on a refreshable braille terminal that Will would have on a desk in front of him."

"That's tight," says Nick.

"Wow, cool," I say, though I have mixed feelings. I hadn't expected Whitford to actually think up a functioning system for this. Now I really have to audition.

"Good luck," says Nick. "You'll need it. I mean, *we'll* all vote for you. But you've got, you know, pretty steep competition. Xander Reusch-Bag has been host for, like, three years."

"Wait," I say. "We have class together. Isn't his last name just Reusch?"

"Well, yeah, technically it's just Reusch," says Nick. "But, hey. If your last name rhymes with *douche,* you really should know better than to also act like one. Otherwise the nickname is inevitable."

• • •

After Nick and Ion head home, Whitford suggests that Cecily and I try out his braille terminal.

Cecily holds an iPhone and I have the terminal on a desk in front of me. I feel the braille and start to read.

"It was the year 3017 and the Doctor was walking through the empty streets of a mysteriously abandoned city floating on what appeared to be a cloud..." I read. "Dude, what *is* this?"

"Doctor Who fan fiction," says Whitford, as if this should have been completely obvious. "You don't like it?

Do you think the scene should've started with him stepping out of the TARDIS?"

"Wait, did you write this?" I ask. "You write fan fiction?"

"Uh...no...I mean, my friend wrote it, I just thought he might want feedback on it," says Whitford.

"Right," I say, completely unconvinced. "Your *friend*."

"Let's keep practicing," says Cecily. "We need to get this down for the audition."

As we continue through the text, the Doctor still wandering around a postapocalyptic wasteland in search of someone called his "companion," there are times when Cecily gets a bit behind or ahead in her scrolling. After a while, though, my reading speed and her scrolling harmonize into the perfect match.

CHAPTER 10

On Monday, at the start of journalism class, Mrs. Everbrook asks everyone who wants to audition for the morning announcements to raise a hand.

I raise mine, wondering if Cecily is raising hers, too. I better not be the only one challenging Xander and Victoria. Cecily better not be backing out. I'm doing this for her, after all.

The way she spoke at that museum—the energy in her voice as she described each painting, her belief that art means something more than brushed-on oils dried and chipping on stretched canvas—that's a voice that deserves to be heard. That needs to be shared. And if I have to audition in order for her to give it a try, then so be it.

But then I return to panicking. I'm probably the only one raising my hand. This was a bad idea.

"Don't try to pull your hand down, Will. I already saw you," says Mrs. Everbrook. "All right, so we've got Xander and Victoria running for reelection, I see. And they will be challenged by Will"—she pauses while scribbling my name on paper, and for a moment of dread, I am sure that I am the only one, that Cecily backed out—"as well as Tripp, Connor, and Cecily."

I exhale in relief. She raised her hand.

"I'm going to go ahead and pair you off as cohosts," says Mrs. Everbrook.

"Tripp and Connor, you guys are buddies, right? I'll make you the first pair. And Cecily and Will, you did great work covering that van Gogh exhibit, so I'll put you together."

Mrs. Everbrook goes over some rules about the audition process, including what to wear. Then she gives us the rest of the period to work on our journalism assignments.

I hear Cecily's footsteps approach and listen as she slides into a desk beside me.

"So we've got a problem," she says.

I turn my head toward her, alarmed.

"I don't own any button-down tops."

"What?" I say, not used to hearing a girl describe her wardrobe as *our* problem.

"Were you listening? Mrs. Everbrook says that's what we're supposed to wear. Nothing else works well with a clip-on microphone."

"Oh, right," I say. "Well, come to think of it, I don't think I have any button-downs other than white dress shirts. That's what my mom always tells me she buys. But Mrs. Everbrook said white looks bad on camera, right?"

"Yeah."

I sigh. Shopping for clothes is basically my least favorite activity.

"Well..." I say hesitantly. "Maybe we could go to the mall together? Help each other pick out an audition outfit?"

I realize how absurd the phrase "help each other" sounds. Like she could use *my* help picking out an outfit.

"Can you go right after school today? Might as well get it over with as soon as we can."

"Sure."

"I just have to get back for a quiz-team practice thing at five, though."

"No problem," I say. "How long can it take?"

•••

Malls are full of hazards: unimaginably large parking lots, shoulder-bumpingly dense crowds, shin-bangingly low fountains. And escalators.

Ugh. Escalators. When it comes to motorized floor transport, elevators are pretty annoying, but escalators are much worse. They are one of those rare obstacles that make me kind of wish I had a guide dog to help. But today I don't need one. I have Cecily.

I tell her, "Okay, put my hand on the rail and tell me when to step forward. On a count of three."

She does.

"One...two...three," she says. I step. "Oh, no, no, no, you're on a crack, move back, move back!"

I step backward, only to land on the flat part of the moving floor, which is steadily sliding out from under me. I feel myself losing balance, tipping...but Cecily stops me from behind and shoves me upright.

"There," she says. "Now you are standing on a step. Hold still."

I notice the feeling of her hands against my back as I regain my balance. Her palms and fingers are small but firm against the fabric of my shirt.

As we go up, the scrolling motion of the escalator reminds me of Whitford's braille terminal.

"Listen, Cecily, if you'd rather have another cohost, I can drop out of the audition," I offer.

"No, you can't drop out," she says.

"I don't think you need me anymore," I say. "You can do this on your own."

"No," she says. "I mean, *neither* of us can quit. I already tried to switch partners."

That feels like a slap, but before she can explain, she tells me we are at the top of the escalator, and disembarking requires both of us to concentrate.

We go into a Forever 21—it has a small men's section, Cecily says—and she picks out a few shirts for me to try on and finds some for herself before heading for the fitting rooms.

"It's a long line," Cecily warns.

We stand in silence for a while, stepping forward every few minutes.

"What's wrong?" she asks.

"Nothing," I say.

"You seem upset."

"I'm fine."

"Why don't you tell me what's wrong?"

"What do you care?" I snap, displaying more anger than I mean to.

"I'm...your friend. I'd like to help."

"How could I *not* be upset? You just told me you tried to dump me as soon as you heard we were paired together today."

She's quiet for a while. Synthesizer-heavy pop music pulses out of speakers above us.

"Will, I asked to be switched to a different partner because I want you to win."

"What are you talking about?"

"I told you. I'm just not the kind of person people would vote for to be on television first period every day. But it doesn't matter anyway. Mrs. Everbrook said once we raised our hands, there was no dropping out, and once she assigned partners, there was no questioning her 'infallible matchmaking.'"

I say, "No way. *You're* the one who would carry this team. As a blind person, I consider myself an exceptional judge of the human voice. And you, Cecily, have a lovely voice."

We listen to the next five tracks of ceiling music in silence. But the beats sound happier than before.

"Jeez, it's almost five o'clock," says Cecily.

"Already?"

"Yeah. I'm supposed to be back at school in twenty minutes."

"We can just leave."

"No, we waited this long. Might as well just try these on and buy something as fast as we can. I'll text our adviser that I might be late."

Even after we finally make it to the front of the line, we wait another ten minutes until one of the dressing rooms finally becomes available.

"Thanks for your patience," says the employee working the area. "Which of you is next?"

Knowing we're short on time, I turn to Cecily.

"Tell me if this is too weird," I say. "But want to just share a room to save time? I can't, you know, watch you or anything."

She hesitates for a moment. Okay, maybe too weird.

But the employee cuts in.

"I'm sorry, we have a strict one-person policy."

"Well—I'm blind," I say.

"Oh," she says. "I guess that's all right, then."

People will accept blindness as the rationale for all sorts of exceptional behavior.

"Cecily?" I ask.

"Yeah, I guess that's a good idea. It'll be faster, like you said."

From the reverb of the door clicking shut, I judge the fitting room to be about two arm lengths across.

"I don't need the mirror, obviously, so you can stand in front of it," I say.

"Okay," she says.

We shift around in the small space, bumping into each other.

I listen to her slide her T-shirt over her shoulders and drop it on the floor. I'm not going to lie: I am immediately on high alert, my senses piqued.

When referring to bikini models or whatever, I always hear that certain parts are "left up to the imagination," and those are the parts that are especially intriguing.

Well. Just think if it was *all* left up to the imagination.

When I suggested we share a fitting room, I was just trying to save time. I didn't anticipate I'd be so, well, *turned on* by the experience. After all, I can't actually imagine what I've never seen. But now...the idea that I'm standing so close to this girl who is in the process of changing shirts...mere inches away from my own body...

I try to control my quickening breath, hoping she doesn't notice. I don't want her to think I'm a perv or something. And I don't want her to think I like her, you know, in *that* way. This is just hormones. I'd feel this way under these circumstances with any girl getting undressed mere inches from me. Wouldn't I?

CHAPTER 11

The news comes the next day when Mom picks me up from school.

"Will!" she shouts as soon as I get in the front seat of the Tesla. "I have the best news! Dr. Bianchi's office called. Your B-scan showed you are a candidate for the surgery!"

"Wait. Why did you talk to them? I told you I wanted to handle this myself."

"I *thought* you would be excited," she says coolly.

"Don't try to turn this around on me. We had an agreement."

"I haven't even told you the best part yet."

I know she's hoping I'll take her bait—*Oh, now I'm excited, Mommy, tell me the good news, please, please!*—which is exactly why I say nothing.

Eventually she gives in. "Fine, I'll tell you anyway. They have a stem cell donor!"

I can't help myself. "Really?"

"Really."

"Already?"

"Already."

"How long do I have to decide?"

"What do you mean, *decide*?"

I pause as it sinks in. "Don't tell me you already scheduled the surgery."

She says nothing.

"You did, didn't you?"

I hear her shift uneasily.

"Didn't you?"

"I'm sorry...I didn't...Why would you need to decide anything?"

I'm furious. This is *my* decision. Not Mom's. I can't believe she would just schedule it herself. Or actually, I can. I can totally believe it. It's just like her.

"We had a deal!" I say. "I'm canceling it."

"Will, you will do no such thing!" she snaps.

"Try and stop me," I say. I tell Siri to call Dr. Bianchi's office. A receptionist answers.

"Hi, this is William Porter," I say.

"Will! Stop this immediately!" Mom says.

"My mother spoke with your office earlier to schedule an operation. I'm going to need some time to think about it first—"

"William Porter, hang up that phone!"

"So I would like to put that operation on hold."

The receptionist confirms my request and says they can give me time to decide, but that if I want to move forward with this opportunity, I need to get back to them by Monday.

"One more thing," I say. "Please make a note on my account that my mother, Sydney Porter, is not authorized to speak with your office on my behalf."

The receptionist explains that since I am a minor, I can't prevent my mother from speaking with their office about me.

But since Mom is hearing only one side of the conversation, I reply, "Great. Thank you for making a note of that."

The receptionist counters that she did not make note of that, as she said, I am a minor—

"All right, thanks, bye!" I say, and end the call.

The car is quiet for a while.

"You didn't have to do that," says Mom eventually. She sounds more hurt than angry.

"We had a deal. You went behind my back."

We ride the rest of the way home in silence, without even normal car noises to cut the tension. Teslas—making awkward car rides even more awkward since 2008.

• • •

Dad gets home soon after we do. There's a knock on my door.

"Will? Can we go for a bike ride on the tandem?"

I know Mom sent him as a proxy to persuade me to have the operation. But a part of me wants to be talked into it. I do want to see, after all. So I agree.

We put on our helmets and push out of the driveway. Once we are a few seconds away from the house, he says sternly from the front seat of the bike, "Your mother told me about the incident earlier."

"I just felt like I needed some time to think it over."

"I think that's extremely wise."

Wait, what? This was not the talk I was expecting. "You do?"

"That's why I wanted to take you on a bike ride. I disagree with your mother on this, so I needed to get you alone to hear my concerns."

He's right. If Mom overheard Dad disagreeing with her like this, she'd flip out. He wouldn't get in a single word.

Dad continues, "Since we first heard of the operation, I've been researching the medical literature on the subject. I have to say, it doesn't look good, Will."

"Is that a pun?"

My dad is a serious man, so I know that it's not. I just like to mess with him sometimes.

"Um, no, sorry, no pun intended."

He warns me that we are going to take a left turn. After a few seconds of pedaling, I know we are passing Whitford's house.

He returns to his speech. "In all of recorded history,

there have been fewer than twenty documented cases of early blind gaining eyesight later in life. And in those twenty cases, the outcomes were quite poor."

"You mean, like, it didn't work?" I ask.

"No, those twenty are the few on whom it *did* work. But they all had difficulty recognizing certain objects for the rest of their life. Some of them lost their vision again later. More important, every single patient experienced major depression as a result of gaining sight."

I make a point to push harder on the pedals so Dad won't notice how unsteady and confused I'm feeling.

"They were depressed? After they could *see*?"

"Yes. Some had mental breakdowns. Many wished they could return to blindness or even considered deliberately damaging their own eyes. Most were reported to have undergone significant changes in personality, usually toward melancholy and sadness."

"But why?" I ask. "That doesn't make any sense."

"The world didn't look as good as everyone told them it would. One of the most famous cases, a man in England, was devastated to discover that both he and his wife were not as good-looking as he had always assumed they were. He was in otherwise good health, but he died just nineteen months after seeing for the first time. Apparently, he simply lost his will to live."

I try to reverse the dark tone of the story. "Dad, is this your way of telling me I'm really ugly?"

He doesn't take the bait. "No, son, I'm trying to say—"

"I know what you're trying to say. It was just a joke."

We ride in silence for a few seconds.

"Right turn."

As I feel the bike lean into the turn, my mind swirls with this new information.

I want it to work. I want to find a way to make things turn out differently for me. "But what if I—what if a person went into the operation with low expectations? About what everything looks like?"

"That would be wise, of course. There are other obstacles, though. You'd also have significant frustration while adjusting. Your visual cortex has developed atypically."

"Dr. Bianchi said that my brain could rewire itself," I counter.

"Maybe. But only after a very difficult adjustment period. Listen, Will, I don't want to come across like I don't believe in you. I think you have adapted tremendously well, and that's exactly why you *don't* need this surgery. For instance, where are we right now?"

"What?" I say, confused by the sudden topic change.

"Where are we in the neighborhood?"

I've been keeping track of the route as we ride. "The front gate is coming up on our left," I say.

"Correct," he says in a Proud Father voice. "And you know this without ever having seen a map of these streets. You know our location by estimating the distance and our speed and tracking our turns. You already have a rich life, and you are perfectly capable of functioning in society."

"I guess," I reply, as if to say, *So what?*

"I myself figure out where we are by looking up from the handlebars and taking in the entire scene all at once. That's the thing, Will. You're a skilled navigator now, but if you have the surgery, it will be like starting over."

"What do you mean?" I say.

"When a blind person sees for the first time, it's not like he can suddenly process everything going into his brain. He can't identify faces, people, shapes, or colors. You'll have no point of reference for understanding the images. Slight left."

"So it's like a foreign language, then?" I ask, adding, "People learn new languages all the time."

"Not exactly. For an adult born blind, learning to see would not be like learning a new language, it would be like learning language itself for the first time."

Dad alerts me to an upcoming bend in the road. But I'm not paying much attention and find myself startled when the bike tips and accelerates through the turn.

"And, Will," he adds, "that's if the surgery is successful at restoring your vision, which still requires immunosuppressant drugs that could allow you to die of something like a cold or the flu."

That seems to be his trump card. Not only will the surgery not work, but even if it does, I might die of the flu.

Really subtle, Dad. "Well, I guess we know which side you are on here."

"I'm on *your* side, Will."

We coast a bit in silence, and I feel the breeze biting my face.

He adds, "I think you are a tremendous son, and I couldn't be more proud of you. I just don't know why you'd want to risk everything on this operation when you already have so much going for you. Think about it this way: What if instead of giving *you* sight, this operation made a clone of you. The clone had functioning eyes, but in order for it to live, you had to die. Would you agree to that?"

This strikes me as kind of extreme. "Come on, Dad, that's totally different!"

"Is it, though? Because currently you are a blind person. With sight, you would be a sighted person. If you gained your sight, by definition, you'd be a different person than you are now."

"I guess," I agree reluctantly.

"So the Will that is riding this bike with me would no longer exist. You would be a different Will. Who would that Will be?"

I count out a few seconds as we ride, his question hanging unanswered in the air.

"We're home, aren't we?" I ask.

"That's my son. That's my Will. See what you can already do? What would you need this operation for?"

I go back to my room and lie on my bed and think it over. When I first heard about this procedure and had my initial appointment with Dr. Bianchi, I immediately thought, *Yeah, I want that*. But after what my dad just said, I'm not so sure.

CHAPTER 12

As I waste stomach space ingesting large quantities of pointless beta-carotene at lunch the next day, my friends and I discuss the homecoming dance. Ion suggests I go with Cecily.

Be the only blind person at a school dance? Um, no thanks.

"I don't think that's a good idea," I say.

"Why not?" she asks.

I don't want to tell her that I'm afraid of the event itself, though, so I share a different problem. "Well, for one thing, I came to public school to learn how to live independently. I don't have time for a girlfriend right now."

"Who said anything about a relationship? You can just go as friends. But if it makes you feel any better, Cecily doesn't want a boyfriend."

"Why not?"

"You'd have to ask *her* that," says Ion. "But seriously, what could better demonstrate how well you're mainstreaming than taking a girl to homecoming?"

"You have a point," I concede. As an afterthought, I add, "What does Cecily look like?"

"What do you mean?" asks Ion.

Her hesitation is a surprise—usually people jump at the chance to paint word pictures for me.

"You know, like, is she pretty or whatever?" I clarify.

"Does it matter?" asks Ion.

"If she's pretty? No, not really."

But sort of. I mean, I know it shouldn't matter. I'm just curious. And the way Ion's stalling, I'm beginning to think the answer is no.

Whitford jumps in. "It's not like that. Cecily is more of a sister to all of us. We don't see her in that way."

It's obviously a nonanswer. Even if you don't think of her like "that," you would still notice if she was pretty. Wouldn't you? I think so. Isn't that how eyesight works?

I always kind of assumed Cecily was pretty. Her voice is pretty enough. But maybe I was wrong. Again, it's no big deal. I'm just curious.

Nick says, "If you guys won't do it, I'll be the one to tell him."

Ion tries to interrupt. "Wait, Nick—"

"She's hot," he continues, undeterred. "Totally."

There's a pause.

"Yeah, all right," chimes in Whitford. "It's true. I mean, I've only got eyes for my girl Ion here, but if I was single, I would definitely look twice when Cecily walked by."

"Ion?" I ask.

"Cecily is lovely," she says slowly, carefully.

"So you think she'd say yes? If I asked her to homecoming?"

"I don't know, actually," says Ion.

"So you are trying to set me up with a girl who might reject me?"

"Didn't you just say you are trying to learn to live *independently*?"

"Yeah, but—"

"Well then, find out for yourself."

• • •

Two days later is the first round of auditions. I wear my new blue button-down shirt.

The announcements begin as normal. But after three minutes, Xander says, "Well, my fellow students, we have reached that exciting point in the year when you all decide who will have the distinct honor and privilege of bringing you your announcements every morning beginning in the spring semester. This year there are three teams of potential cohosts: team one, which is myself and Victoria; team two, Will Porter and Cecily Hoder; and team three, Tripp Atkinson and Connor Forthright."

I feel so nervous it's like there's a balloon expanding in my stomach and pressing against my insides. I told Cecily, and she said not to worry about it. Being nervous was perfectly understandable. I was shocked by how calm she sounded. Honestly, I wanted to drop out. But her voice brought me back, and here I am, getting ready to go on camera.

"And now team two will take over the next section of today's announcements. Good luck to all the teams!" says Xander. He sounds sincere. Almost.

Cecily and I take our seats at the anchor desk. I feel heat from the studio lights on my face. I angle my head in that direction, knowing the lights are positioned near the camera. I'm wearing my glasses so people will assume that I'm making eye contact with them on their screens.

"Good morning, I'm Cecily."

"And I'm Will."

Cecily begins a flawless read of her first announcement, about the canned-food drive next week. I'm filled with dread. I know I'm going to screw this up for us. I'll probably puke all over the camera.

My fingers are in the ready position on the braille terminal. This is it. I'm about to read my first announcement.

When Cecily finishes the details about the food drive, I hear her hand move quickly to the iPad in her lap, where she scrolls the teleprompter to the next announcement. As she does, I feel the braille letters refresh under my fingertips.

I begin to read aloud, like a kindergartner nervously sounding out words for the first time. "Tickets for the homecoming dance are—"

At this point, there's a gap in the text where the next word should begin. Three empty characters instead of one space. Which is weird.

"—still for sale in the main—"

The line of text refreshes, but it begins with another set of three blank spaces. It's quite distracting, these typos.

"—office for only ten dollars. Get yours—"

I hit another empty slot where a word should be. What's going on here? Reading braille aloud is difficult enough if you are, say, in your bedroom all by yourself. But I'm on camera in front of a thousand pairs of eyes for an audition. And now I have to deal with problems in the script? Is there a glitch in the program? Or is Cecily not scrolling correctly?

"—today so you don't miss out on an unforgettable night this Saturday."

I hope my face doesn't show how upset I am. I'm speaking like a person who barely knows the language.

Everyone probably thinks I'm nervous. Like I'm stuttering because the whole school is watching. Or maybe they think I'm a slow braille reader.

I want to stop reading from the script and say, *This is not my fault! I don't know what's going on here, but there's something messed up with the script, not me!*

I *knew* this wouldn't work. I knew I shouldn't be auditioning for a position where my performance is entirely reliant on other people to hold their own. Lean on others long enough, and eventually you'll fall. And in these auditions, I'm falling hard, crashing and burning in front of the whole entire school.

It also occurs to me that if I could see, none of this would've happened. My reading would have sounded just as smooth and confident as Cecily's.

As soon as our part of the broadcast is over, we return next door to Mrs. Everbrook's classroom. Cecily and I sit together while we wait for the announcements to end. Tripp and Connor begin their audition on the classroom television.

I whisper to Cecily, "When you were scrolling through my script, could you see those gaps between words?"

I'm trying not to sound as accusatory as I feel.

She pauses, then whispers back, "Those weren't gaps."

I'm confused. "They felt like gaps on my braille terminal. I wasn't sure what to say. I don't understand. What were they?"

"Don't worry about it, Will," she says, as if she's speaking to a child or something. Which only makes me feel worse. First I look stupid on the announcements, and now Cecily acts like she's doing me a favor by not telling me why?

"What *were* they?" I repeat, frustration creeping into my voice.

"They were images," she finally says.

That's not the answer I was expecting. "What kind of images?"

"They were, like, emojis. But not the normal ones," she says reluctantly.

"Meaning?"

She shifts uncomfortably in her desk. "They were, I guess you could say, X-rated emojis. Of, like, human... anatomy and stuff."

"Why did they show up as blanks for me?"

"Maybe your terminal doesn't translate emojis."

I consider this. "That's probably lucky. If it had, I would've read..."

"Some very inappropriate-sounding announcements, yes."

None of this makes sense. "But why were they only in *my* script? I can't even see them. Why not yours, too?" I ask.

"Oh," she says, "they *were* in mine."

"But your reading was flawless! How did you read them without getting distracted by the, um, you know..."

"That's the advantage of being bullied all your life, I guess. You get pretty good at tuning that kind of thing out."

I feel ashamed. Here I was, partially blaming Cecily for my audition going poorly when it had probably been much more distracting for her.

"I'm sorry," I say. The words aren't really enough, but they're all I can think of. I'm sorry about everything— sorry that I was awkward in our audition, sorry that I was blaming her for it, and sorry that she, apparently, has had to put up with stuff like this for years. "I'm really sorry."

"Don't be."

We sit there quietly for a moment, listening to Tripp and Connor read from their own script. Now that I'm paying attention, I hear tension in their voices, like they are about to burst out laughing. Could be the nerves. Or maybe their script got tampered with, too.

"You think they have the same problem?" I whisper to Cecily.

"Looks that way," she agrees.

I sit back in my desk and wonder if maybe I did a *better* job reading the announcements because I couldn't see the images. Maybe my blindness actually helped me rather than hurt me. For once. And maybe there are other times in my life when this happens without me even realizing it.

I ask, "Did Xander and Victoria's script have the images? They sounded normal."

"Yeah, but they've got a few years of practice, you know?"

"So who would've done it?" I ask.

"Probably just some hacker wannabe trying to impress his hacker wannabe friends."

But then Xander walks by—all three of the teams have been hanging out in Mrs. Everbrook's classroom this morning during tryouts—and he leans in between our desks.

"Nice try, noobs," he says. "In live broadcasting, you have to be prepared for anything. I hope you learned that lesson today."

"Wait," says Cecily. "You put those in the scripts on purpose?"

"Who, me? I didn't say that. I just said I hope you learned something today."

After he walks away, I whisper to Cecily, "You think we have any chance of making it to the final round next week?"

"Honestly? Not really. Not with me—"

I interrupt, "Don't say stuff like that. You were great."

Cecily doesn't answer at first. Then she says, "Thanks." It sounds like the compliment really meant something to her. I decide to seize the moment and take Ion's advice.

"Hey," I say, "you got any plans Saturday night?"

"Um...no," she says.

"Want to go to homecoming? With me, I mean?"

"Uh, yeah, sure."

"Just as, you know, friends?"

"As friends?"

"Or cohosts. If you prefer."

"Whoa, let's take things one step at a time," she says. But I can hear that she's smiling.

CHAPTER 13

On Saturday, as she is driving to my house to pick me up before homecoming, Cecily calls my cell.

"Are you all ready?" she asks.

"Yep."

"Wanna just meet me outside?"

"My mom really wants to get a photo of us together. Can you come in? Just for a minute?"

"Oh..." She pauses. "Yeah, sure, of course. Okay, I'm parking in the driveway now."

She hangs up, and I go to the front foyer. The doorbell rings, and I reach out and turn the knob. My parents are crowding in right behind me, apparently in a competition to find out which one of them can make this situation more awkward.

I swing open the door.

"Wow," says Cecily. "You look great."

I'm wearing a suit and tie. I even allowed Mom to comb my hair for the occasion.

"So do you," I say. "At least, I assume so. Let me ask my parents. Cecily, I would like you to meet my mom and dad."

They don't say anything. This is awkward. So, so awkward. What's wrong with them?

"Oh," says Mom. "Hi there."

Hi there? Seriously?

"Hi," says Cecily quietly.

"It's so very nice to meet you," says Mom, trying to recover.

I guess Mom and Dad are just as nervous as Cecily.

"Well, how does she look?" I ask, trying to bring back the festive mood I would've expected in this conversation.

There's another pause. Dad says, "She looks gorgeous, Will. Absolutely gorgeous. It's wonderful to finally meet you, Cecily. We've heard so much about you."

I hear them shake hands.

"We've got a dinner to get to," I say. "Mom, you want to get that picture?"

"Wait, I brought you a boutonniere," says Cecily. "Want me to pin it on?"

"Sure," I say.

She comes close. Her perfume floats in through my nostrils and fills my whole body.

"Careful, don't poke him," Mom says. I feel her lean toward us.

"Would you...like to do it?" offers Cecily.

"If you don't mind," says Mom.

Cecily steps aside as Mom's perfume enters my personal space, filling me with quite different emotions than Cecily's did.

"There," says Mom. "You look so handsome. And here's Cecily's corsage."

I reach my hand out to accept the floral arrangement, but instead hear Mom sliding it onto Cecily's wrist herself.

"Can we take the picture now?" I ask, feeling increasingly eager to ditch my parents.

Mom arranges us in a few different poses and, once satisfied with her photo collection, dismisses us.

"Be safe," she says.

"Have fun," adds Dad.

We go out to a fancy dinner with Whitford and Ion, and then go to the dance, which is in the school gym.

"I'm gonna show these folks how to dance," says Whitford as we walk through the doors. "We'll meet you out there."

Ion and Whitford walk away, leaving the two of us standing by ourselves.

"I'm nervous," Cecily says. The music is loud, and she has to put her lips right up to my ear so I can hear her. I feel her breath against my skin, warm and humid, like a breeze in the summer. It gives me chills, having her face so near.

"I've never been to a dance before," Cecily continues. I feel her leaning away, as if shrinking back toward the exit. "I don't know if I can do this. I don't know if it's a good idea," she says.

I reach down and give her hand a supportive squeeze.

I remove my sunglasses and turn my head so my mouth will be close to her ear. She's so close that my chin bumps lightly against her hair. "Keep your eyes on mine. Don't look away. It's just you and me."

I give her hand another squeeze. "Got it?"

Her head brushes against my face as I feel her nod.

"Then let's go dance," I say.

We turn toward the music. She walks slightly ahead, our fingers still intertwined. If someone saw us and didn't know better, I bet they'd think we were a couple, walking together, holding hands.

As we move across the gym, the music gets louder and the bodies closer.

"How's this?" she says, yelling above the music.

"Perfect!"

This is not my first school dance, but it *is* my first dance at a mainstream school. I try to start dancing, bouncing my shoulders and arms to the beat. But I feel self-conscious, like every student in the gym is staring at me, judging my inability to dance. If I could *see* my dance moves, and if I could look at everyone else to compare myself, maybe I wouldn't feel so insecure. Everyone else, everyone who can see—I know they aren't having such doubts. But I try to pretend I'm confident and having fun because I want Cecily to be comfortable.

"So . . . are you dancing now?" I yell at her.

"Yeah! My moves are incredible. Shame you can't see them!" she jokes.

"Let me feel them," I say.

"What?"

"Come closer!"

I reach out both of my hands, and she lays her fingers across them. It's a fast song, a club remix of a pop radio hit. I tug on her arms, and she steps one of her legs right up against mine, and then the other, her whole body following so that we press together from the ground up, like a closing zipper, until our faces meet, cheek to cheek. She wraps her arms around my neck, and I pull against the small of her back, tighter with every beat of the song. The silky fabric of her dress is stretched taut between her legs. I feel the strap of her camera, which is hanging over her shoulder even now, at this school dance and in this dress. I love that about Cecily. Always ready to capture beauty.

That's when I realize something: I want to kiss Cecily.

But does she want to kiss me?

If only I could see her, read her expression, look into her eyes. Then I would know.

I let my mouth brush over her ear.

She doesn't pull back. That's a good sign. Maybe there is something here. Something more than friendship. Something more than cohosting.

Suddenly a great holler rises up from the crowd, a collective protest. The music is still going, but I get the sense that everyone has stopped dancing.

"What just happened?" I say.

"The lights turned on," says Cecily.

"What? They were *off* before?" I ask.

"Yeah."

"So we've been dancing in the dark this whole time?"

"Pretty much."

That's not what I had imagined. I generally assume that wherever I go, there is light. If it was dark, people would stop moving. Wouldn't they? They'd get confused and start stumbling over each other. They'd be, well, blind. But apparently, it's been dark at this dance the whole time.

"You mean, people danced when it was dark, but when they could see themselves, they stopped dancing?"

"I guess you could say it that way. Oh, wow, the lights—this is a perfect shot."

Her camera lens pops off, and she starts clicking away.

"The students' expressions of frustration and unhappiness juxtapose with the formal attire and decorations..." She's narrating, like an art-museum tour guide, when there's a sudden cheer. I feel the vibrations of the crowd returning to their dancing.

"Let me guess. The lights are back off?"

"Yep."

But that moment before—when I was really considering kissing her—has passed.

• • •

After the dance ends, the four of us change out of our dress clothes and go to Mel's Diner and get a booth. It's pretty much the only place open twenty-four hours a day in our town, and based on the volume of chatter inside the restaurant, it seems every other teenager at that dance had the exact same idea we did.

"Room for one more?"

It's Nick's voice.

"Well, look who it is!" says Whitford.

"Scoot over," Cecily says to Whitford. There's some sliding, and Nick sits down on the other side of the table from Cecily and me.

I smile. "I thought homecoming was for sellouts?" I say.

"This isn't homecoming. This is the after-party," Nick says.

"Who's up for an after-after-party at my place?" says Whitford. "Maybe a game of Settlers?"

"We can't play Settlers on a *Saturday*," I say.

Cecily pokes me. "It's past midnight, silly. Now it's *Sunday*. Very, very early Settlers Sunday."

We go to the Washingtons' house and play till six in the morning. I eat so many Skittles I think I might be sick.

"I can just walk home from here," I tell Cecily on the front porch. "It's right around the corner."

"I've got something else in mind," she says. "Are you free for a drive?"

"Sorry, can't," I say. "I have several predawn appointments on the calendar."

"Very funny."

She takes us to Mole Hill Park, and we walk up what seems like a million flights of stairs to the top of the hill this place is named after and sit down on the grass.

"You know this used to be a volcano?" she asks.

"And we're sitting on top of it right now?" I ask, slightly disconcerted.

"Don't worry, it's not active anymore."

"Hey, can I take a picture of you?" I ask.

"Of me?" she asks.

"Yeah. You're always taking mine. Seems only fair I should get a turn."

"I prefer to stay behind the camera," she says.

"Oh, come on," I say. "Just one photo."

"Fine," she says, handing me the camera and guiding my finger to the shutter button.

"Say cheese!" I say.

"Seriously?" she says flatly.

I press the button, and the camera clicks. I do it a few more times.

"Okay, that's plenty," she says, taking the camera back.

"Why are you supposed to say cheese?" I ask.

"I have no idea," she says.

"Nick would probably know," I say.

"Probably," she agrees.

I hear her move and sense warmth near my hand, as if her own hand is hovering nearby, thinking about grabbing mine.

Do it. Please. Grab my hand.

But then the warmth is gone. She must have pulled away. "Anyway, I wanted to take you here because this is the highest point in the city. So it's the best place to watch the sunrise."

First we almost kissed on the dance floor. Now we almost held hands. Or at least, I think that's what happened. And if so, she definitely *chose* not to hold my hand.

I guess it's like Ion said: Cecily's not looking for a boyfriend. And hand holding can definitely lead to boyfriends. Not to mention kissing. I guess it's a good thing the lights came on during the dance.

"Sunrises," I say, turning my attention back to the present. "I don't get it. They get all this hype. I mean, *I* rise out of bed every morning when my alarm goes off, but no one climbs mountains to watch and rave about how beautiful I am. What's so great about a sunrise?"

"All the colors. So many blended together."

"Like a painting?"

"Yes, but better."

"Why better?"

"It's bigger than a painting, for one thing. It's infinite, in a sense. A sunrise stretches across the whole sky, and behind it is the entire galaxy and the rest of the universe."

"Well, that's something," I admit, leaning back and feeling the grass with my fingers.

"Plus, a painting is only a representation of the thing. But a sunrise . . . a sunrise is the actual thing."

I shift my weight on the ground. "I'm not trying to be cynical or difficult," I say. "But why does a multitude of colors make it beautiful? Like a multitude of smells. Well, that's like the cafeteria at school...and that's not something I'd stay up all night and walk up that many steps for, I'll tell you that."

She chuckles. "The colors work together; they don't compete. It's not like the cafeteria. You know how it is at Thanksgiving dinner when there's all those smells from so many dishes, but they mix together into something wonderful?"

I imagine the scent and find my mouth watering. "Mmm, yeah."

"Or you could use sound as an example. The hallway at school is noisy, right? A cacophony of noises banging together. But a sunrise is more like an orchestra. Many different instruments harmonizing to create beautiful music. Does that make sense?"

I catch the wonder in her voice, and that, more than the words, lets me understand her meaning. "Yeah, actually, it does."

"So can you imagine a sunrise now?" she says hopefully. It makes me cringe a little, how earnestly she believes I am capable of imagining a sunrise. I don't want to disappoint her. But I don't want to lie to her, either.

"Honestly?"

"Honesty would be preferable."

"In that case, no." I try to say it playfully soften the blow of disappointment for her.

"Come on!" she says, touching my arm "Just try."

"It's impossible," I say. "I'm sorry. I really wish I could."

After a beat, she asks hesitantly, "Can you imagine me?"

"Yes. I can."

She seems pleased by this. "How?"

"I've sensed you. I've felt your arm when you guide me. I've heard you speak, smelled your perfume tonight..."

I've kissed two girls in my life. One at the school for the blind. One at blind camp. My understanding is that people usually close their eyes just before contact is made, which makes kissing the closest Cecily and I can ever come to having an identical, shared experience: both of us feeling our lips touch, both doing so without sight.

"Do you want to touch my face?" she asks. "Would that help you see me?"

"Yes," I say. "It would help a lot."

She sits up and places my palms against her cheeks. I run my fingers over her skin, sensing the smoothness of her forehead, the texture of her eyebrows, the delicacy of her eyelashes, the resoluteness of her nose, the smallness of her lips, the downward angle of her chin.

She's beautiful. There's no doubt about it. And I want to tell her that. I'm so tempted to blurt it out. And—I want to feel that face against mine.

But I can't. Kissing would only make things complicated. Really, really complicated. What would we be, cohosts with benefits or something?

I remove my hands from her face and lean back in the grass.

I hear Cecily's camera.

"Photographing the sunrise?" I ask.

"Of course," she says with a note of humor in her voice. "I need some hype-worthy photos for my collection."

CHAPTER 14

On the Monday after homecoming—the day I'm supposed to make a decision about my operation—Mrs. Everbrook calls me over to her desk.

"Will, I understand you have a mighty interesting opportunity," says Mrs. Everbrook.

"What do you mean?"

"The experimental surgery."

I'm confused. "How do you know about that?"

"Your mother called me this morning, said we should run a story about it."

I feel my skin grow hot all over. "My mom called you?" Of course Mom wants the paper to run a story about it. To get me to choose the operation because of peer pressure.

"Yep. Figured I should check with you first."

I groan. "I can't believe her. She's so...so..." I struggle for words. "No, don't print an article."

"It stays between us, then. You and Cecily have that bus driver interview today, right?"

"Yeah."

"Then hop to it."

But a thought occurs to me. One way or the other, I do have to decide today. And in front of me is one of the few adults that I trust to give me unbiased advice.

"Mrs. Everbrook, before I go..."

"Yes?"

"Do you think I should do it? The surgery?"

She pauses for a moment, considering her answer. "I think you're the one who will have to live with the decision. So no one else should make it for you."

"Thanks, Mrs. Everbrook."

"Here's your hall pass," she says. I reach out, and she puts the slip into my hand.

Cecily guides me as we begin our walk to the side parking lot to meet the bus driver. All the other students are inside classrooms, so our footsteps echo in empty hallways.

"My B-scan results came back a few days ago," I say. "I'm a candidate for the operation."

Her pace seems to slow for a second as she takes this in.

"Don't you still need a stem cell donor?" she asks.

"They already found one. I have to decide today if I want to do it."

She says nothing. The only sound is the squeak of our rubber sneaker soles.

Eventually I say, "I sort of expected you to be excited. If it worked, I could see colors and nature and everything."

"Yeah, no, I'm really excited for you," she says unconvincingly.

"But?"

"But nothing. It sounds great."

We walk through a set of doors.

"I can hear it in your voice. You think it's a bad idea."

"Not bad, just risky."

"There are risks, true," I concede. "Including a risk I could see for the first time."

"That was the risk I was talking about."

This surprises me. "Wait. You don't *want* me to see?"

"It's not that. More like...I think there could be unintended consequences to being able to see. Side effects, you might say."

"Such as?" I ask.

"It's like how people often feel worse about themselves after they have plastic surgery," she says.

"Because the surgery went wrong?"

"No, because the surgery went *right*. They look better on the outside, but inside they have the same self-image issues as before. And that's a problem no operation can resolve."

I'm about to ask why she knows so much about plastic surgery when she stops our movement.

"We're here," she says.

She opens a door to the outside and greets the bus driver, who is waiting for us on the sidewalk. He's friendly.

And old. I can feel his age when I shake his hand, and I can hear it in his voice. Also, there's the fact that he's been driving a bus for our school system for forty-two years. He's finally retiring. That's what my article's about.

I listen to Cecily pose him a few different ways around a bus—leaning up against it, sitting in the driver's seat, that sort of thing.

After the photo shoot ends, he asks, "Either of you want to take her for a spin?"

"No thanks," says Cecily.

"I'm blind," I say.

"No problem by me," he says. "I can direct you."

"Really?" I say.

"Today is my last day. What are they going to do, fire me?" He laughs heartily.

"All right, sure," I say. I've always wanted to try driving, and a school bus seems as good a vehicle as any.

"Will, I'm not sure this is a good idea," says Cecily, tugging at my arm. I shake off her hand and reach forward to locate the entrance to the bus. I climb the stairs. The driver stands and helps me find the seat.

"Put your hands out like this—there you go, that's the wheel. Now use your right foot to find the pedal. Nope, that's the brake. A little to the right. Very good. Okay, that's your gas. You'll press very slowly on that when I say go. You coming to join us, missy?"

"No, thank you," Cecily says, obviously displeased with this plan.

"Take some photos of this!" I say.

"I will do no such thing," she says.

"All aboard!" says the driver. I hear a sound of air hissing and then the noise of the outside is gone. He's closed the door.

"You sure this is a good idea?" I ask.

"We all got to start somewhere. Forty-two years ago, I had never driven a bus, neither."

"But you could see."

"That's true, that's true. We'll just go slow. And I'll keep a hand on the steering wheel so you don't hit anything. Okay, now press real gentle with your foot like I talked about."

I do, and the *rut-rut-rut* of the engine rumbles all around us.

The bus driver laughs.

"Are we moving?" I ask.

"Yes! You're driving a school bus!" he says.

I laugh, too.

"Whoa, whoa, whoa, a little less gas."

I let up a bit.

"Turn coming up. This is the hard part. Let up all the way on the gas. When I tell you, turn the wheel to the left. Ready...now!"

I spin the wheel a little. "More! Turn it more!" I do. "Hold it there!"

The force of the turn pulls me slightly to the side, like when I'm riding in a car and it's going around a corner.

But now I'm not riding in a car. I'm in a *bus*. Also, I'm driving. That's kind of different.

It's way different than a tandem bike, where, sure, I have the sensation of movement, but the front rider is steering. Here, I'm in control. I'm moving fast and I'm driving a big heavy machine and it feels amazing. It is freedom and independence and control, not just of myself but of something much bigger than myself.

People with driver's licenses must feel this way, like, every day. They probably don't even notice how cool it is. And if I have the operation, I could get a driver's license. I could drive a bus or a car or the front side of a tandem bike. And if I did, I would never forget to notice how good it felt. I would always remember what it was like to be without that freedom, and I would appreciate it every time I grabbed the steering wheel or the handlebars and looked at the open road ahead.

After we complete a lap around the parking lot, he takes over at the seat to put on the parking brake and cut the engine.

"That was real good," he says. "You're a natural!"

"Thanks."

"I hear there's a job opening up around here. Maybe you should apply?"

I laugh.

The hissing sound comes again, letting in the outside air. I walk down the stairs.

"Did you see that, Cecily?" I ask, giddy with excitement. "I drove a school bus!"

"Yes, I saw," she says dryly.

"That was so cool!"

She gives a sort of *humph* sound. I ask the driver a few questions for my article, recording our conversation on my phone, and then Cecily and I begin the walk back to the classroom.

"Can I ask you a personal question?" I ask Cecily once we are the only ones walking the corridor.

"If you ask it, do I have to answer it?"

"Not if you don't want to," I say.

"All right."

"That first day of school," I say. "How come you cried because I was staring at you?"

She hesitates. "What do you mean?"

"Now that I know you better, it just doesn't seem like you."

"I'd just had a big fight with my mom that day before school," she says. "I'd been crying already and was just on edge. And when I thought you were staring at me, it just set me off again."

"I'm sorry," I say. "Are you close with your mom?"

She laughs mirthlessly. "No, we don't really get along."

"What about your dad?"

"Yeah, he's much better than my mom, but they're divorced. I only get to see him a few times a year."

"Where does he live?" I ask.

"In Los Angeles," she says, her voice becoming more cheerful. "Near Venice Beach. He has this little yellow bungalow on a corner lot. There's always a bright red surfboard on the front porch."

"Does he surf?"

She laughs, for real this time.

"No, it must've come with the house or something. The closest he comes to exercise is watching football on TV," she says.

"He doesn't even go to the beach?" I ask.

"Sometimes, but he *drives* there. It's, like, six blocks away, and he refuses to walk," she says. "I'm always telling him to get in shape, but he doesn't seem to listen."

We walk in silence for a while. On a long, empty stretch of hallway, I hear two sets of footsteps approaching. Just as they pass us, a male voice says, "Hey, look! It's Batgirl!"

And then there's a cackle of laughter and the smack of a high five.

An intensity of feeling like I've never experienced shoots through my body. Anger, raw and pure, and the knowledge that I must fight, I must hurt, I must destroy the owner of that voice. I drop Cecily's arm and whirl toward the sounds of their laughter, letting fly an arm trained by years of swinging a cane, a fist strengthened by a lifetime of touching and gripping. But my hand only breezes through the air, and the force of the swing knocks me off balance. I nearly topple to the floor.

The misfire of my punch just makes me angrier. I spread my arms out wide and charge toward where I last heard their laughter, hurling myself with the intent to bring anyone in my path to the ground. Instead, I run face-first into something metal. I bounce off with a pop and land on my back, losing my balance for real this time.

"Oh, Will!" says Cecily. She's already crouched beside me, and I can hear that she's crying.

What I don't hear is anything from the boys who passed us in the hall. There's no jeering, no laughter, nothing. They just walk away. And that's what hurts the most, so much deeper than the smack to my face when I hit what must've been a wall of lockers: that my attempt to fight doesn't even warrant mockery. It's not serious enough even to be made fun of. I lost myself in rage and set my mind for combat, and it resulted in exactly nothing.

I'm shaking with anger. They called her Batgirl because she's associated with me, because she was walking with me, and I'm blind. Like a bat. They ridiculed her for being my friend, and I couldn't stop them.

And that's when I come to two realizations. Number one, I will have the operation. I want that freedom I felt driving the bus. The freedom to move through the world without a cane. I want that every day. And I want to experience the pigments on a painted canvas and soak in the texture of a sunrise. I want to examine every floor tile in the hallway at school and watch water gush out of the faucet in a bathroom sink. I want to see it all; I want to savor every fiber of this other layer of reality.

And number two, I recognize that I had a weirdly strong reaction to those guys. I'm not the kind of person who usually gets in fights. So why did I swing at them? There's only one possible explanation, one that I've been trying to ignore but now must admit to myself: I am definitely falling for Cecily.

CHAPTER 15

The stem cell transplant happens three days later, on Thursday. I had my tonsils removed when I was a kid, so this is not my first time under anesthesia. This first operation, then, doesn't feel like a big deal. And it's not like I'll wake up being able to see. I have to wait for the second operation for that. Until then, I will wear bandages under my sunglasses. My eyes will be sensitive from the trauma of the transplant and need protection to heal.

Mom comes with me. She wouldn't take no for an answer this time.

Dad isn't here. Well, actually, technically he is in the same building. Working. Tying up some old guy's testicles or whatever he does. He said he couldn't reschedule his operating room time today, but I think he's really just unhappy with my decision and didn't feel comfortable being here.

I go to the operation prep area, and Mom and I sit down, me on the hospital bed. A nurse slides a curtain around us, the hooks grinding along their track on the ceiling until the fabric surrounds us like a little bubble, dampening slightly the sounds from the rest of the room—soft voices, whirring machines, beeping monitors. Several different people cycle through, asking me a bunch of questions to make sure I'm not allergic to anesthesia, that I don't have a history of breathing problems, I haven't eaten in the last twelve hours, and on and on. Each question implies a potential complication, something that could go wrong. And these aren't even issues related to eyesight; they are just the general risks of surgery. I'm starting to wonder if maybe Dad was right, maybe there are too many risks here, and I can feel my heart racing as they put the IV in my arm. Then I start to feel really good, just relaxed and calm. Mom strokes my hair like I'm five years old, but I don't even care, because I feel wonderful and I love my mom.

• • •

The next thing I know, I am waking up, the beeps and whirs slowly coming back to life in my awareness.

"Honey?" says Mom, apparently noticing I'm awake from the movements of my hands (it's not like she can see my eyes opening after all, not with these bandages over them). "How do you feel?"

I feel great. Pain meds are awesome. I should have surgery more often.

"Fine," I say.

It's an outpatient surgery so Mom drives me home that afternoon. Over the weekend, I just chill. As the medicine wears off, my eyes start to hurt more and Mom's doting starts to get annoying, so I spend most of the weekend in my room, poking around the Internet on my laptop.

• • •

During morning announcements the next Monday at school, Xander reveals that the schoolwide votes have been tallied for the first round of auditions. Tripp and Connor are eliminated. Cecily and I advance. We have our second and final audition Friday.

Mrs. Everbrook gives Cecily and me a copy of the script in advance, and we spend the week practicing so we can memorize it ahead of time instead of reading it on air. Unlike the first audition, where we just sat behind the desk, the next one includes a green-screen segment.

Victoria hosts that segment for Xander and herself, standing in front of a green wall that, Cecily explains, runs through a computer that makes the background look like something else. Apparently it's the same technology meteorologists use on television to show maps of weather patterns. It all means nothing to me. For now.

Xander wraps up their audition with a reminder to cast votes for their favorite pair of hosts during lunch. The winners will be announced in a few weeks. Then it's our turn. Cecily begins with a few announcements from the desk and then tosses to me at the green screen, where I'm standing wearing my usual sunglasses. No one knows the bandages underneath are from a surgery that may soon result in eyesight. For now, I'm still just the blind kid. I launch into my thirty-second explanation of the upcoming school renovations. A series of floor-plan diagrams is appearing behind me, and I point out different areas as I speak.

"A little higher, now to the left—perfect," says Cecily in my ear.

Last night we decided that I should be the one to do the green-screen segment. Because it's the exact opposite of what everyone would expect. The blind kid standing in front of a green wall—a color he's never even seen—and gesturing at imaginary pictures as if he knows where they are. It seems like the perfect trick to get people talking about us, and maybe even voting for us, too.

Just as we practiced yesterday at his house, Whitford gave me a wireless earpiece that he said looks something like a hearing aid. From off camera, Cecily turned her television mic off and turned on another hidden mic that sends a signal to the device in my ear. That way she could direct my hand movements as I recited the script, and all the while I look like I know where I'm pointing. Pretty clever, right? We thought so.

At lunch everyone agrees that we nailed the audition.

But the winners won't be announced for a few more weeks. By then, I will have already had my second operation. Or not, depending on whether they find a cornea donor. My future, or more specifically the future of my eyesight, lies with the destiny of one unfortunate organ donor. Somewhere out there right now, presumably, is a healthy person looking through a pair of functional corneas with no idea of the future that awaits him. I wonder what he's looking at right now. A spreadsheet at work? A documentary on Netflix? The cracks in a sidewalk? He could never imagine that in a matter of days, someone else will be looking through those very same eyes. Or maybe it's a she. Either way, something calamitous will have to occur in order for those corneas to become available to me. Is it wrong for me to hope for such a thing?

CHAPTER 16

The weeks tick by slowly. First I have to wait a month for the stem cells to (hopefully) be accepted by my body and begin to replicate into daughter cells. I still go to school, do my journalism work, hang out with my friends, and sometimes with just Cecily. But I never really feel completely there because in the front of my mind, right behind my eyes, in fact, is the uncertainty of my future. After the month of healing is up, it's a waiting game. There's a two-week window in which I can receive a transplant. If no corneas become available, game over. The procedure fails. So the wait is painful, that buzzing anxiety even louder in my mind. It's tough to concentrate at school or on my homework. They seem so mundane compared with the breathless narrative of my mind. I sit in my room and jump at the slightest sound, hoping it's the telephone with the call from Dr. Bianchi's office. Finally, after almost two weeks, just as my window is closing, the call comes. A donor has been found. My corneas are en route.

This is a strange feeling, discovering that I might gain a new sense. I've gone my whole life without eyesight, assuming that I wanted it, assuming that my life would be so much better if I had it. But now that it might possibly happen, I'm actually kind of afraid. Afraid of all the stuff that could go wrong, the complications, the side effects, the chance of infection. And there are the difficulties adjusting that Dad told me about. The possibility of confusion, stress, headaches, depression.

Who will I be when I am no longer Will Porter, blind teenager? What will I be like? And the other kids in school—the hundreds of voices I pass by each day in the hall—what will they think? To me, they're an undifferentiated and anonymous mass of chattering, but to them I must be memorable. I mean, I'm the only blind kid in the school. The one with the sunglasses and the long white cane that swings shin-whackingly wide through the hallway, the guy who occasionally makes wrong turns, who uses the girls' restroom, and who's trying to host the morning announcements. Will they think that I am a sellout, giving up the life I was meant to live, the body I was born with, not accepting my place and my condition and my community? Or will they accept me as one of their own, without question?

Cecily comes over and sits with me in my room the night before my operation. "You know what bothers me?" I find myself telling her as we sit beside each other on my bed. "Blind people have a difficult time because most people have eyesight. But if the whole human race had evolved *without* eyesight, we would have adapted to it. Like bats. That species figured out how to survive without it."

"Bats?" That word seems to catch her off guard.

"Yeah, like bats. I mean, sure, if the entire human race went blind all at once tomorrow, the world would fall into chaos. But if it happened very gradually, we'd figure it out. We'd find a way."

"I guess," she says reluctantly.

Then I realize what I'm hearing in her voice: She's remembering the incident in the hallway, when those guys called her Batgirl because she was hanging out with me. I don't want her pondering the price she's paid for being my friend, so I abandon the bat example and move on to a different line of reasoning, speaking quickly to distract her.

"You probably think blindness is really difficult, but that's just because you have adapted to your situation. That would be like if Superman looked at you and he was like, 'Cecily's life must be so terrible because she can't fly.' He's only saying that because *he's* used to flying. He doesn't know that you can get along just fine with the abilities you have as a normal human."

"Are you having second thoughts?" she asks, interrupting my train of thought.

"I guess. Maybe. I don't know," I say slowly. "I mean, sure, I'm fine the way I am. But I think things could be better."

142

"Like because you'd enjoy seeing things?"

"Yeah," I say. "And I'm tired of the way people treat me. Like the way people are so overly nice to me because they assume I can't do stuff for myself." I pause, thinking back on the Incident. "And sometimes the opposite. Sometimes they're...cruel."

"What do you mean?" she asks.

So I tell her the whole story. About Alexander, about Candy Land, about my parents' decision to send me to the school for the blind.

"And after that," I conclude, "I eventually realized I just couldn't rely on other people. Maybe that sounds stupid."

"It's not stupid," she says. "I've had a hard time trusting people, too, because...well, I was bullied a lot when I was a kid."

I pause, waiting for her to elaborate. "You want to talk about it?"

"Not really."

It's quiet again, and eventually she says, "Do you want me to take your picture?"

"With bandages over my eyes?"

"Just in case you want to look back and see what you looked like before."

"Not really, thanks. But can I take a picture?" I ask.

"Of what?"

"Anything. How about my savory wall?"

"All right."

I hold the camera in front of me, and she flips out the

monitor so she can see the picture. She directs my aim and takes my hand in hers, guiding it to the lens. She lets go so I can adjust the focus myself, but I wish she had kept her hand on mine.

"Rotate slowly, slowly, right there. Now press with your pointer finger."

I do and hear the familiar snap of the shutter.

• • •

That night, I barely sleep. When I do, I dream about Cecily. I can see her, and it's very strange because I'm not actually *seeing*. Still, this one feels different from my usual dreams, which are just hallucinated representations of my everyday experience, loosely chronological narratives of touch, sound, and smell.

Dad takes the day off so he and Mom can accompany me to the hospital. Which must suck for him, using a vacation day to go hang out at his place of work.

The three of us sit in a waiting room for a while. Mom fills out my paperwork. I wonder what it will be like when I can fill out my own paperwork. I hear Dad shuffling through the newspaper. I imagine how it will feel to read with my eyes. I run my fingers over the upholstery of my chair and wonder what color it is. Sure, I could ask Mom. Or I could use my iPhone app that identifies colors. But that's not the point. I don't actually care what color the chair is. I just want to be able to determine it at a glance. Like a normal person.

144

We are called into another room and go through the same pre-op conversations as we did six weeks ago for the stem cell operation. The anesthesiologist asks me a million times if I'm allergic to anything. He knows Dad, and they exchange pleasantries. Dr. Bianchi comes by for a final check-in. He says he is hopeful the operation will succeed, but he reminds me that "we cannot predict outcomes with certainty." The stem cells have been in my eyes long enough now to have created daughter cells, which will hopefully get my retinas to function. The stem cells are like a foundation, he says, and the corneas are like the house. Assuming my body doesn't immediately reject the new corneas, it's possible I might be able to sense light as soon as he takes the bandages off after this operation.

The anesthesiologist puts an IV in my arm. He tells me things are going to get blurry. I start to remind him that I won't know the difference, but I'm fast fading into sleep and the words get stuck in my throat.

• • •

All of a sudden, there's this incredible noise pounding into my brain. It's louder than anything I've ever heard, like a jet engine, endless, incessant, painful. It sounds like static, feels like a continuous slap to my face, and tastes like acid.

"AHHHHHH!" I yell. "Turn it off! Turn it off! Turn it OFF!"

"Will! It's Mom! It's okay. It's okay."

I struggle to move and find my body still lagging behind my brain's commands.

"TURN IT OFF!" I yell, gaining enough control to thrash and jerk.

"Nurse!" Mom says. "Nurse!"

Some more words are spoken—I hear "sedation"—and the sound gets foggy, and I fall asleep. When I wake up again, it's back, pounding me, demolishing me, demanding my attention.

"The sound! Turn off the sound!" I say.

"Will, sweetheart, calm down!"

"Mom?" I say, my hands groping, finding her face. "Mom, make them turn it off!"

"Turn off what, Will?"

"That sound!"

"There is no sound, Will. It's very quiet in here."

"You can't hear it?" I ask desperately.

"No."

"Dad?"

"I don't hear anything, either, Will. What does it sound like? Are your ears ringing?"

And that's when I realize that the sound is not coming through my ears. In fact, it's not actually a sound at all. It's something else, some other sensory fist pummeling me with its volume and intensity. *Is this eyesight? Have the bandages already come off? Am I seeing? Is this my very first sight?*

But I lift my hands to my eyes and find bandages. If my eyes are bandaged, what could I be seeing? Unless...is this what the inside of bandages look like?

No, my eyelids are shut. I can feel that. They are taped closed by these very bandages.

What, then? What is this?

Then I remember how once Mrs. Chin explained that complete blindness is not like a person with normal eyesight covering his eyes. Because even then, that person still sees darkness. Blindness is like trying to look at the inside of your shoe through the bottom of your foot. It is an absolute lack of sensory input.

And that's when it hits me: I'm seeing darkness for the first time.

My heart starts to pound from excitement. I can hear it on the monitor, which just proves to me that I'm right. What I thought I heard before wasn't sound.

"OH MY GOD!" I say. "I can see! Mom! Dad! I can see!"

"Honey—" Mom says sympathetically.

"No, really! I can!"

"You still have bandages over your eyes, sweetheart," she says. "I'm sorry."

"No, that's just it! I can see the darkness! I can see the blackness! It's unlike anything I've ever felt!"

I don't know how to describe it to them. Metaphors rush through my mind: It's like a new arm is growing out of my face and getting electrocuted! It's like I have a second nose and it's snorting wasabi!

"Oh my God, Sydney, he can see!" says Dad. "His retinas are transmitting to the optic nerve! They are sensing the absence of light!"

Mom and Dad start laughing, and so do I. We laugh and laugh, and Mom starts crying, and the laughs and cries blend into each other. But none are louder than the sound of the blackness pouring into my brain from my eyes. I keep telling myself, no, it's all right, this is a good thing. But my brain keeps saying, *What is happening? What is this mass intrusion of static?* The overload of sense from my eyes, plain and dark though it may be, is so strong that I can barely pay attention to Mom and Dad. Eyesight is asserting itself as king over my other senses. It is enacting a coup d'état against hearing, smelling, tasting, and touching. And I can already tell it's going to be a bloody revolution.

CHAPTER 17

The next morning, on Friday, Mom takes me to Dr. Bianchi's office to get the bandages removed.

At the medical building, Mom and I walk back to a little examination room.

"Mom, can you just wait outside?"

She doesn't say anything. She's stonewalling, trying to guilt me with her silence.

For a moment, I consider the situation from her perspective. I think how special this moment must be for her. Her blind son is about to see for the first time. How many parents get to witness something like that?

"Fine, you can come in," I say.

"Thank you," she says, sounding genuinely appreciative.

I sit down on the crinkly paper of the examination table, and we wait in silence for Dr. Bianchi. After about ten minutes, I hear the door swing open, and he says, "How is my star patient feeling?"

"Pretty good," I say. "But there's a lot of weird stuff going on."

I tell him about the pounding darkness, about what I assume are the first transmissions from my upgraded eyes to my brain.

"That means it worked, right? I will be able to see?"

"Possibly, possibly. Although this will take time to develop. You will come back to see me on Monday and we will begin your therapy. For the weekend, just rest and take note of what you experience."

I hear him scrubbing his hands in the sink. He walks over to me and starts to tug at the tape gripping my temple.

My mom is quiet. Too quiet. "Mom, are you video-taping this on your phone?"

She says nothing, which tells me I'm right.

Dr. Bianchi pauses.

Annoyed, I say, "I don't want all your little friends at the country club crying tears of joy while watching a video of me on endless loop. Turn it off."

"William, this is a moment you will treasure forever. You will want to show it to your own children someday! And your grandchildren!"

I know that "you will treasure" is Mom's code for "*I* will treasure," but hey, in the history of the world, fewer than twenty mothers have seen their blind child gain sight. Why not let her enjoy it the way she wants to?

"Fine," I say. "Keep filming."

"All right. But I am starting a new recording now. I don't want that little, um, altercation on the video."

"Whatever," I say.

Dr. Bianchi removes enough of the bandages that I am able to lift my eyelids. But my view still seems to be blocked by the remaining gauze.

This is it! I'm about to see!

I try to slow down my excitement so I can soak in every detail. This is a moment I want to remember forever. This is the moment I go from blind to seeing. This is the moment I step into the light.

Dr. Bianchi has stopped peeling back the bandages. I feel his face move very close to mine.

"Why did you stop?" I ask. He says nothing. "Dr. Bianchi?" Still he doesn't reply. "Can you finish taking off the bandages, please?"

He steps back. "I'm sorry, Will," he says.

"What? Is something wrong?"

"The bandages are already removed several moments ago. Your eyes are open and blocked by nothing."

I blink. I feel my eyelids move up and down, just as they always have done when I blink. And I sense that raging current of black noise that I have felt since yesterday. But there is nothing more. There's nothing else that signals of color or movement. I close my eyes and press them tightly shut. Then I open them. Nothing different: It's the same sensation whether my eyes are open or closed.

"Turn it off!" I say. "TURN IT OFF!"

"Do you hear the noise again?" asks Mom. "It's quiet in—"

"No, the camera! Turn it off!"

"Oh, yes, sorry," she says quietly.

I grab at the paper cover of the examination table with both hands, fingernails clawing through it, ripping it, balling it into my fists.

"Delete it, Mom! No one can ever see that video! Ever!"

"I already did."

I feel my lower lip quiver. I'm about to cry. (My eyes may have never performed their primary function, but my tear ducts have always worked just fine.) No, I will not cry. I'm sixteen years old. I won't cry in front of my mother and my doctor.

"Let's go," I say. I have to leave. I have to leave immediately and go home and lock my door and sit in the darkness and never come out.

"Wait for one minute, please," says Dr. Bianchi. "You must allow me to examine you."

"It didn't work, can't you see that?" I spit the words at him. "Can't you *see* that with your *eyes*?"

"Will, I gave you the warning about how the cortex must take time—"

I stand and put my hand out, a signal for Mom to give me her arm as a guide.

"We're leaving," I say.

Mom is as upset as I am. I can hear it in the way she

snatches her purse and jumps to my side, ready to lead me out of the office.

In the car ride home, I hear her sniffle.

"Are you crying?" I ask, rank hostility in my voice.

"Of course I am."

"*I'm* the one who can't see!" I say. "What are *you* crying about?"

"Don't you know how hard this is for me?"

"How hard it is for you?" I demand. "For you? Why is everything always about you?"

"No, Will, it's about you. It's hard because I can't do anything for you. It's hard because I would give anything to be able to switch eyes with you, but I can't."

That wasn't the response I expected, and it shuts me up. I want to be angry at Mom, but I can't be. It's not her fault. The surgery was her idea, sure, but I chose it. I wanted it.

Once we get home, I go to my room and shut the door. I cry and punch things for hours. I break some stuff. I don't even know what. Just random stuff.

The absurd part of all this, I realize, is that I am now so much worse off than I was before the operation. I had convinced myself I wouldn't be one of those people who got depressed when the sight of the world wasn't what I expected. But I went through everything, two surgeries, and I didn't even get that far. I was blind two weeks ago, and I'm still blind now, but at least before I was relatively happy with my life. I was adjusting to a mainstream school, had friends, a possible cohosting gig, good grades. I had it all, really. And then I got this fantasy that I could have sight, that I *should* have sight, and it made me feel like what I had wasn't enough anymore.

That's why I had the operation.

And guess what? It didn't work. I'm still blind. And it's worse, too, a more unbearable blindness. Before, my blindness felt like nothing, and now I have this loud static in my brain that offers only distraction and pain.

Dad was right. I'm a different person now. The operation *did* change me. It changed the way I see my life, from the inside. Now I know I will never be happy as a blind person. Now that I have had a sample—not of full eyesight, per se, but of believing that it could be mine—and then had it ripped away from me, I will be forever stuck in this twilight world of dissatisfaction.

My phone buzzes intermittently. Just-checking-in-on-you texts from Cecily, Ion, Whitford, and Nick. But I don't want them to know. I'm not ready for them to know. I'm not sure I'll ever be.

I spend the rest of the day wallowing on the floor with my door locked, not even coming out for meals.

CHAPTER 18

When I wake up Saturday morning, I am immediately assaulted by insanity.

It's like music, except with a thousand different instruments that are all out of tune. It's like the taste of every food group at once, like the smell of all the cafeterias in the world.

Am I having a nervous breakdown? Am I dying?

And then I move my head, roll it to the side, and everything changes. Now it's a completely different swirl of madness.

I blink.

And it all shutters for a second, shakes like an explosion inside my brain. I blink again, another explosion, like a single blow to a bass drum, like jumping into an ice-cold lake. I close my eyes, and the overload regresses, simplifies itself back to that pounding darkness I've experienced for the two days since the surgery.

I open my eyes, and the flood pours into me again,

choking me with its power. I shudder, from my feet to my head, and it all changes again, shakes like an earthquake. I start to feel dizzy, and I fall on the floor, and my head gets lighter—*this is it, I'm dying*—and without warning I feel my stomach empty itself up through my throat. Vomit spills all over my face, and I recoil, which changes the world again. Then I'm coughing, and with each gasp, the torrent changes. I blink.

BOOM.

It breaks over me, a tsunami-level wave of sensory input.

I know it, deep down, below gut level, in the deepest region of my instinct.

These are colors.

I can see.

The colors shake and tremble, move in and out like a radio with a spinning dial. I retch again, bucking with the force from within. Compared with that pounding darkness I was experiencing, this is so much faster and louder and more stupefying. It's like nothing I've ever experienced, a nonsequential mishmash of percolating aliveness.

The colors shimmer. They shift. They *move.*

I can see!

My eyes are working!

These are colors, and they are moving every time my head moves, and I can see them move, and I can see colors and movement!

"Mom!" I yell. "Help! Come quick! Moooooom!"

Within seconds, she bursts through the door. At the very moment I hear the sound of the door opening, there is a violent change in the colors, and seeing it causes me to heave once again.

"Oh my God, Will, what happened!?" she cries, her feet rushing toward me, the colors moving so wildly now that I close my eyes and fall backward. "Henry! Henry! HENRY!" she calls for my dad.

"No, Mom, it's all right!" I say. "I can see! I can SEE!"

"Henry, call 911!"

"Listen, Mom!"

"Henry, get an ambulance! Something is wrong with Will! Oh my God, my poor baby, what is happening, what is that all over you?"

"No, Mom. Listen to me—"

"What is it—oh my God, Will, what happened?" says Dad, his voice going from loud to earsplitting.

Mom is hysterical, screaming from all directions at once. "Did you call an ambulance?" she yells.

"No, I—here, I will do it right now," says Dad in a panicky voice I've never heard before.

"Dad!" I say. "Stop! I'm fine! I just threw up! That's it."

"What?" he asks, a little calmer.

"Look at me! I'm fine. It's just puke. That's all," I say the words slowly, emphasizing each one, trying to get my parents to slow down and listen.

But my eyes are closed. I can't let in the colors. They are too much. They overwhelm me; they're drowning me.

"What's wrong with your eyes?" asks Dad.

"Call the ambulance!" Mom is still screaming.

"What?" I ask. I try to open my eyes again, just a little.

"Your eyes—why are you squinting?" says Dad.

"Because, Dad. Because I can see!"

"You what?"

"HENRY, DO SOMETHING!"

"I can see, Dad! I see colors and movement! I can't open my eyes, because it makes me dizzy. That's why I threw up."

"Oh my God," he whispers. Then he snaps into action. "Sydney!" She keeps screaming about the ambulance. "SYDNEY!" I hear him grab her, hold her still. "Stop! Stop! He can see. Will can see!"

She quiets down, and after a long pause, says almost reverently, "Will...you can...you can see?"

"Yes, Mom, I can see!"

I hear her collapse on the floor and start crying. But they are tears of joy. I can hear that much. Tears of joy.

"Can someone get me a towel or something?" I ask. "I need to get cleaned up."

I take a shower with my eyes tightly shut, afraid to let in the overwhelming power of new sight. After drying and dressing—with my eyes still closed—I make my way to the kitchen table by touch. Mom and Dad gather around. I open my eyes.

"Well?" says Mom. "What do you think? Do we look how you expected?"

"Uh..." I say.

I'm not really sure how to explain it. It's not that my family doesn't look how I expected. It's that they don't look like anything at all. Or rather, I have no way of knowing which part of the soup of color and movement represents their bodies. Each splash of color bleeds into the next.

I do notice certain movements while Mom is talking. Is that her face? Or is it the ticking grandfather clock on the wall by the door? Or the bubbling goldfish tank? Or any number of other moving objects in the room? I start to feel dizzy again and have to close my eyes. I don't want to return to the puking.

"I have no idea what you look like," I say. "I don't even know what a human being looks like."

"But you've *touched* people," interjects Mom. "You know how we are shaped."

"By touch, yes. Not by sight."

I hear something slide across the table. "Here, let's start with a simpler object," Dad says. "I've put it right in front of you. Open your eyes."

I do. I see a churning mass, each color bleeding into the others.

"Recognize it?" Mom asks.

"That's what I'm saying. I don't know where to look. I don't even know *how* to look," I say.

"You sure you don't know what it is?" says Mom.

"Know what *what* is?" I retort.

"There, right in front of you!" says Mom, as if by the intensity of her voice she can compel my pupils to focus, to rewire the nerve connection between my retinas and cortex. "Look where I am pointing! With my finger!"

"I don't think you're quite getting this. I don't know where you are pointing. I don't know what pointing looks like. I don't know what a finger looks like."

"You have fingers on your own hand!" says Mom.

She's right. I do have fingers. I lift my arms, putting my hand out like I am going to shake with a new acquaintance. At the exact same moment I make the movement with my arm, I perceive a shimmer of color, and a resulting surge of nausea passes through me. I gulp down the impulse to throw up again.

That shimmer: It must be my hand. Or my arm. Some part of my body, moving through my field of vision. It is my first glimpse of myself.

I close my eyes again.

"Hold it right in front of my face so I can see it," I say.

Mom picks up the object, and I sense it just in front of my face. I open my eyes. It's obvious the scene has changed, but I can't tell in what way exactly.

"You don't recognize it?" she asks, shocked.

"Not at all," I say.

"Touch it," she says. I put my hands out and touch it. It takes less than a second, less than a millisecond.

"A saltshaker," I say. "It's the saltshaker we keep on the kitchen table."

"This is what I was telling you about before the operation," says Dad. "Object recognition is not instinctual. You will have to learn how to identify objects by sight in the same way you've learned to do it by touch."

"Oh, hush, Henry," says Mom. "This is hardly the time for I told you so."

"Fine, but I did warn him," says Dad. "Color perception, however, *is* instinctual. Maybe you should start there?"

"Do we have any Skittles?" I suggest.

Mom's voice is excited. "Let me get some."

With my eyes still closed, I hear Mom go fetch a pack of Skittles from the cupboard where she keeps the candy stash. She tears it open and pours its contents—*clink clink clink*—into a cereal bowl that she places on the table in front of me. I reach in and pick up one of the candies. I hold it under my nose, eyes still closed.

"Lemon," I say, sniffing.

"Right!" says Mom.

I open my eyes. Every color bubbles in every direction. Which one is the Skittle?

"Hold it closer to your eyes!" suggests Mom.

I close my left eye and move the candy immediately in front of my right. There's an earthshaking shift of color as I move it so near.

"That's yellow," says Mom.

"Yellow," I repeat, examining the hue. "I always expected yellow would be...quieter."

Mom and Dad laugh. And then I do, too.

I go through each flavor like this: strawberry (red), orange (the only flavor with the same color as its name), apple (green), and grape (purple). I try to associate each smell and taste with its color so I can remember it. But as soon as I close my eyes, the colors meld into a psychedelic rainbow in my mind, and I can't remember which one is which.

"Pop quiz," says Mom, and I look at one of the candies she holds close to my eye.

"Uh..." I say. "Orange?"

"No, it's green apple," Mom says, disappointed.

"Go easy on him," says Dad. "He's never learned his colors before."

I practice with Mom and Dad until I can correctly guess the color of the Skittle about half the time.

More important, the dizziness seems to be settling down.

"Let's try some objects," Mom says. "Real fruit. Much healthier than candy."

"I don't think he's ready for shapes," says Dad.

"Of course he is," says Mom.

I hear several pieces of produce plop down in front of me. Simultaneously I notice a change of colors. I could be seeing either the fruit rolling onto the table or any movements Mom and Dad are making. The world is nothing more than a confusing cascade of living color, an infinitely large waterfall of Skittles pouring out in front of my eyes.

"There," says Mom. "Do you recognize any of this fruit?"

I stare blankly, trying to home in on the fruit that is now apparently in front of me. But all I can sense is the pulsating chromatic glow coming at me from every direction. I have no idea where to look to find the fruit.

"Your eyes will probably cue in on movement," says Dad. "Here, son, I'm picking up a piece of fruit now and waving it. Can you see it?"

I observe a flux of color, a yellow ripple in my perception. What fruit is yellow? A lemon. But we don't keep lemons in the house. What else?

"A banana!" I exclaim.

Mom squeals with delight.

"Can I touch it?" I ask.

Dad places it in my hands, and immediately it becomes not just a guess based on color, but a real, actual banana. I know this shape. I know this texture and weight. I know the firm grippiness of the skin, the pointy taper of each end. As I examine it with my eyes, I attempt to record and catalog: This is what a banana looks like.

"How about this one?"

I spot another flow of color darting around.

"It's red, right?" I ask.

"Yes!" says Mom.

"An apple?"

"No," says Dad.

What else is red?

"A strawberry?"

"No."

"A watermelon?"

"No."

"I give up."

"Come on, Will!" says Mom. "You can do it!"

"Sydney, listen to him! He didn't know whether it was a strawberry or a watermelon! He can't even judge relative size," says Dad.

"You know I'm sitting right here, right?" I say.

"He's not identifying the fruit," Dad continues. "He's just guessing based on the color. His brain is not equipped yet for visual object recognition."

"I'm not one of your patients, Dad," I say bitterly. "I'm your son."

"I'm right, though, aren't I?" he counters. "You just saw it was red and listed fruits you know are that color?"

"Of course," I say. "How else do people recognize things?"

He drops it into my hand. I immediately identify the small spherical shape and the protective outer skin.

"It's a grape," I say.

"Right," he says quietly.

"I thought they were green?" I ask.

"They can also be red," says Dad.

"Dad's right," I confess to Mom. "I was just guessing based on the color. Maybe I can't see after all."

"Of course you can see!" says Mom. "You got all those Skittle colors right! You just need to learn your shapes! I taught you shapes once before, and I'll do it again! I'll get your baby toys out of storage!"

Baby toys?

"No, thanks," I say.

"Will, just give it a try!" pleads Mom.

"Whatever. Maybe tomorrow. I'm exhausted. I can't do any more right now."

It's true. Vision is draining. I can barely hold my eyes open now. They close on their own, like heavy automatic garage doors. Fatigue overwhelms me, the result, I assume, of an information onslaught my brain is not used to.

I go to my room and shut the door and close the blinds and curtains. Even so, there is still light seeping in through the window. Bright, confusing, exhausting light. I take the blanket from my bed and, standing on my chair, I tuck it in around the curtains, sealing off the window so my room is totally dark. Peaceful, calming, logical darkness.

It's not as pleasant as the "darkness" of being blind, of course. Now that I've had the operation, there is a constant broadcast from my eyes to my brain, even in pitch-black. But at least in my lightproofed room, that communication is relatively simple. At any rate, sitting alone in the dark like this is the closest I can come to the life I am accustomed to, the life that feels most familiar, the life of a blind person.

I check my phone. Texts from everyone on the academic team asking how I am doing. I compose a group text: "Recovery is going well. But I can't really see much yet. Sight is very confusing. I don't know how you guys handle it."

Cecily is the first to respond: "Can you see this?" I observe a yellow color beside her text, but I have to have Siri read to me to figure out that it's an emoji. A smiling face.

Nick adds, "Can you see... YOUR MOM?"

Whitford: "LOL"

I do some homework for a bit, then I get another text from Cecily. "Just dropped something off for you."

"Why didn't you come in?"

"Your mom. That's not a Nick joke btw."

At that very moment, Mom knocks on the door.

"Cecily just dropped this off," she says, setting a cardboard box on the floor beside my bed with a thud.

"You didn't let her in?" I ask.

"Sorry, I figured you were probably asleep. You need to rest, Will."

After Mom leaves, I open the box and reach inside. It seems to be filled with a disorganized pile of small paper. I pick one up. It's the size of a greeting card. I rub it between my fingers. It's so smooth that it's almost sticky to my touch. My phone vibrates. Text from Cecily. "Come to the window."

I open the window and stick my head out.

"Cecily?" I say in a loud whisper.

"Hey," she says, and I can hear a smile in her whisper. "How you feeling?"

"Okay," I say, angling my ears down to hear her better.

I've been so caught up in all the Skittles and colors and dizzying sensory overload that I had forgotten how nice it is to hear Cecily's voice.

"Did you get the box?" she asks eagerly.

"Shhh, keep it down," I say. "I don't want Mom and Dad coming in and finding us acting out *Romeo and Juliet*."

"Sorry," she says.

"So what's in the box?" I ask.

"They're photos," she says. "Of everything we've done together this fall. So, like, our trip to the museum, homecoming, the sunrise. Every picture I've taken when I've been with you."

I don't know how to respond.

She says, "I know you probably can't recognize stuff in photos yet. But when you can, I want you to be able to go back and see everything we've done together."

"Wow," I say. "Thanks. That's really cool. Are there any photos of you?"

"I do my best work on the other side of the camera," she says.

"What about that one I took?" I ask.

"Oh, that one . . . turned out blurry," she says uneasily.

"Don't worry, I'm neither insulted nor surprised to discover a photo I took didn't turn out," I assure her. "As a photographer, I'm really more of an impressionist."

She laughs a little.

We say our good nights. She says she'll see me at school Monday. I say I will see her then. What I don't tell her is that I have a surprise planned: I'm going to practice all day tomorrow, and if my skills have progressed to board game readiness, I'll be seeing her at Settlers Sunday tomorrow night.

CHAPTER 19

I wake up the next morning alone in my dark room. I sit there for a while, not moving. Then it hits me: Today is Sunday. *Settlers Sunday.* For the first time in my entire life, I have the chance to play a board game like a normal person. If I can learn some basic shapes today, I can play this very night.

I would be able to move my own pieces, make my own decisions. I mean, I wouldn't be able to read the words on the cards, not tonight and maybe not ever—Dr. Bianchi said that people like me rarely learn how to read printed text, which was disappointing to hear. But other than that, I should be able to play in the game independently. Without assistance. On my own.

I walk downstairs and sit at the table where Mom and Dad are eating breakfast.

"I want to learn the other colors," I say. "More than the five basic Skittle flavors I saw yesterday. All the other flavors of Skittles—you know, tropical, sour, darkside—they're all different colors, since they're different flavors, right?"

"Yes," says Dad. "I think so."

"Can you go to the store and get those? So I can learn them, too?"

"Of course."

"And, Mom, can you get out my baby toys from the attic? I want to learn shapes."

She agrees. After they finish eating, Mom and Dad depart on their errands, and I eat breakfast alone with my eyes closed. Soon Mom returns, smelling of dust and old cardboard.

"I'm not sure if you remember this toy," she says, setting a box in front of me. I hear the box opening. Plastic pieces tumble out on the table. "Each shape fits with a corresponding hole in this board. You have to match the shape with the hole, and then you can push it through. Make sense?"

"I think so."

"All right, let's start with this shape. Open your eyes."

I do, and I discern exactly nothing.

"Here, look where I am waving my hand."

A flutter of motion catches my attention. Lowering my head shifts the motion into the center of my field of vision. Bending at the waist to get nearer makes the motion take up more space. The object—presumably Mom's hand— actually seems to grow as I get closer to it. *Maybe that's what perspective is?* Perspective. Which reminds me of Cecily. I'm back in that museum, Cecily teaching me about perspective.

Mom's voice interrupts. "All right, I am going to move my hand away. Look at the shape. What do you see?"

I keep my head still and focus on the mass in front of me, the toy block that is left in place where Mom's hand was waving.

"It's red."

"Very good. What shape is it?"

I look intently. To me it is a mere red blob, shifty, formless.

"I have no idea."

"Look harder."

"How do I do that?"

"I don't know, just keep looking."

I stare for a good thirty seconds. But I have no image data bank, nothing in my memory to compare this image to that would help me understand what I am looking at.

"I really don't know, Mom."

"Touch it, then. See if you can feel it."

I put my hand on the block and recognize it instantly.

"It's a triangle," I say, deflated.

"Yes," says Mom. "A triangle."

"How could I not see that? I know what a triangle is shaped like. I've been touching triangles all my life. How can I not recognize one by looking at it?"

I shake my head and sigh.

Mom says, "You just started, Will. You'll get it. It's going to take time." She gives my shoulder a sympathetic squeeze. "Now, look at the board in front of you. Find the triangle-shaped hole and push the block through it."

I hold the triangle in my hand and search for a similar shape nearby. I look and look and look, but see nothing. Not the triangle-shaped hole in the board, not even the board itself.

Finally I give up on my eyes and reach for the board, which I discover by touch to be standing upright, like a computer monitor. My fingers brush over the cutout holes, identifying each shape in an instant—a square, a circle, and yes, here's the triangle. It's so simple. So easy. How could I not *see* that triangle-shaped hole?

"I have to relearn everything. Everything. Even shapes. Even shapes that I know," I say, more to myself than to Mom. I begin to wonder if maybe the surgery was all for nothing. I mean, sure, I can see. But I can't do anything useful with that vision, and I'm not sure I ever will.

"You're smart, Will. If anyone can do it, it's you."

At this moment, Dad walks in from his trip to the store and sits down at the table. "Don't let me interrupt," he says, and then falls silent, watching me, I guess.

Before I press the triangle through the hole in the board, I examine it carefully. I close my eyes and try to imagine it. A red triangle. I repeat this process several times until I'm sure I've got it. Yes. A red triangle. I know what that looks like. I push the block through the hole in the board, and I hear it plunk down on the table. But a crazy thing happens: Even though I sense the red motion as it falls, and even though I *hear* it land, the triangle itself disappears. I scan the table for the missing block. There are various red masses of unknown shapes. But no triangle. I close my eyes. Can I still picture that triangle? Yes, I can. I know what it looks like. So where did it go? How did it disappear?

"What happened?" I gasp. "Where did it go?"

"Where did what go?" says Mom.

"The triangle! It's gone!"

"No, it's not," says Mom. "It's right here."

I hear her arm slide across the table and see a smudge of red as she nudges one of the blocks.

"See?" she asks.

"No!" I insist. "That's not the triangle I was just holding! I *know* that triangle! I memorized it. That is *not* the same one!"

"Oh," she says. "Wait. Look at it now."

I hear her arm move again. There's a click from one of the blocks, and then—What? How is this possible?—the triangle appears! In the very same spot where just a moment ago sat an indistinguishable red mass, there is now a triangle! Is this how vision works? Is this how shapes work? They disappear and materialize, twist and morph, shift in and out of your field of vision without warning?

"What just happened?" I ask. "How did you do that?"

"Honey," says Mom, "it's a triangle-shaped block, not a pyramid. The triangle was just on its side. So from your perspective, it looked like a rectangle. I just turned it so the triangle shape is facing toward you again."

"Rotated? Rectangle?" I stammer. "How can a triangle look like more than one shape? How can it appear and disappear?"

"It didn't disappear, Will. It was there the whole time. It just looked different because it was rotated."

"Objects change shapes if you rotate them?"

"Yes, it depends on the angle you are looking at them from."

"So how many angles are there?"

"Three hundred sixty. You know that," Mom says.

"So to recognize a single object, I have to learn it from three hundred and sixty different positions?"

"I don't know...I never thought of it that way. I don't think it's that many. But I suppose you will have to learn the shapes of objects from different angles, yes."

"What about people?" I ask.

"What do you mean?"

"Do they change shapes from different angles?"

"I guess so. You might see someone from the front. Or profile—like a side view. Or the back."

"I told you this would be difficult," says Dad, unhelpfully.

I sigh, closing my eyes and slouching in my chair. The idea that something can shift into different shapes depending on where you're standing is a completely new concept to me. Until now, the world has been limited to what I could place my hands on. And what I could place my hands on I sensed from all sides at once. The object did not shape-shift if I rotated it. It still occupied the same discrete tactile points, the same shape of space in my hands.

But vision, I now understand, is so much more complicated, full of so much more information. Not only will I have to memorize every shape, every object, I will have to memorize every object and every shape *from every angle*.

It's a task so overwhelming it makes me want to cry.

Maybe, just maybe, I can learn a few basic shapes from enough angles that I can play Settlers tonight. I can play a board game with my friends like a normal sighted nerd would do on a Sunday night. So I press on, all morning and all afternoon, memorizing the shapes of the blocks, associating the touch sensation of each shape with a new kind of shape, a shape I can see.

Fortunately, the colors come easier. I learn each standard and special-edition Skittles flavor, and by the end of the afternoon, I can identify those colors with close to 90 percent accuracy.

Next stop: Settlers Sunday.

CHAPTER 20

The muscles around my eyelids get tired from closing them so often, which I do to give my eyes a rest and block out the dizziness. Back when I was blind—I say that like it was another era when really it's been, what, three days?—I kept my eyes open all the time under my sunglasses. But now the light overwhelms me if I don't give my eyes a periodic break by shutting them. Mom loans me her sleep mask to wear to Whitford's. It covers my eyes, allowing me to open them without having to deal with their dizzying spatial resolution. Figuring people don't usually wear sleep masks in public, I put on my sunglasses to cover the mask. So now I look exactly as I did before the operation. Just your average blind guy.

My friends don't know I'm coming over. I want it to be a surprise. We've been texting a lot over the past couple of days, but I asked them not to visit or anything. I didn't want anyone seeing me until I was able to, you know, see them. I want to make a good first impression with the new me. I want to completely replace their old image of me as a disabled guy with that of an ordinary teenager who recognizes colors and shapes and plays board games with ease.

I still use my cane to walk to Whitford's house, though. His dad answers the door and shows me into the kitchen. There are gasps when I enter. I recognize one of them above the others: It's Cecily.

Cecily shrieks, "Will!"

"Oh my God," whispers Ion.

"Did it work?" asks Nick. "Can you see?"

I tell them about the last three days, the unexpected difficulties, my slow but steady progress.

"Um, is that a sleep mask under your glasses?" asks Nick.

"It's showing?" I ask. "I thought maybe my sunglasses would cover it."

I explain how I'm wearing it because light and colors can be so overwhelming.

"Wait, so you know colors now?" Nick asks.

"Most of them."

"What color shirt am I wearing?"

This is a test I think I can pass. I take off my glasses and the sleep mask. I blink a few times. The light is disorientatingly bright. I close my eyes.

"Can we turn some of the lights off?"

"Sure," says Whitford, jumping up from his seat to flip a few switches. "How's that?"

I open my eyes. "Better."

I rotate in my chair to face Nick. "You'll have to bring your body right up to my face. I won't be able to pick out your shirt otherwise."

"Jeez, Will, I didn't know we were at that stage in our relationship," says Nick.

Nick stands up and steps closer to me. A single color takes over my field of vision.

"Red," I say confidently.

"HOLY CRAP!" exclaims Nick.

They show me a few more colors, and I get them all correct. Their minds are blown. And mine feels pretty darn good about itself.

"So," I say. "How about a game of Settlers?"

"Let's do it!" says Whitford with a clap of his hands.

"Should we set up the map?" I ask.

Awkward silence.

"Will, we already set up the map before you got here," says Ion.

"You can't see it?" asks Nick, confused.

"I...well...I can see colors, and I know some shapes, but it's hard for me to identify objects," I confess.

"Can you see me?" asks Nick.

I swallow. "No, I can't really pick out people yet."

"Don't worry about it," says Ion. "Let's roll to see who goes first. Will, do you want to do the honors? The die is right in front of you."

It's thoughtful of her to tell me where the die is. But even so, the concept of "right in front of me" is vague at best. Furthermore, I know a die is small, and small equals hard to see. If I can't pick out a person, how will I ever see a die on the table?

I look around for it, but all I see is the usual waterfall of colors. I am able to identify them better now than I could yesterday—there's blue, that's green, here's brown—but I can't pick a small die out of the background.

"Here," says Nick, picking it up and placing it in my hand.

I know he's just trying to be nice, and I appreciate that. I mean, Nick's not exactly known for his niceness. But at the same time, it feels like a regression. When I was blind, he never would have handed me a die after Ion had just told me it was right in front of me. Nick would have known that I could simply reach out and find it with my fingers.

"Thanks," I say, trying to sound grateful but probably not pulling it off.

I roll the die and hear it tumble across the table. And as I do, I lose track of it. It disappears into the vortex of my confusing vision, one tiny white cube among millions of pixels.

"Can you see it?" asks Nick cautiously.

It pains me that I can't, and that my friends are now realizing that I can't.

"Uh...well, I can see movement better than stillness. Can you wave your hand over it?"

"Like this?"

I see the blur of white that must be Nick's hand.

"Yes. Great."

I stand up and lean over the table, pressing my nose almost to its surface so the die becomes large.

"Found it!" I say. It's ridiculous, pretending this is a victory after Nick just showed me exactly where it was.

"Can you..." Nick says. "Can you see the number?"

The number of dots. Here's something I should be able to do. After all, the dots on a die are kind of like braille. I've been reading dots all my life. Surely I can count dots on a die.

Except that I can't.

It's not that I can't *see* them. I can see the white square of the die, and I can see little black circles on it. But the dots wiggle and shift when I try to count them. *One, two...* but then I can't figure out which dot I was looking at, and I lose count.

This is absurd. Now I can't count? Toddlers can count! I'm sixteen years old. How am I unable to *count* up to a number of dots between one and six on a stupid little piece of plastic?

"I...I..." I stammer.

They say nothing.

"I have to go home."

I grope around the table with my hands, searching for

my sunglasses and sleep mask. No reason to bother trying to find them with my eyes. That could take all night. Touch is much faster, much more natural. I find the objects and stuff them in my pocket, close my eyes, and flick out my cane, hurrying out the front door before anyone can argue.

Cecily follows and calls after me.

"Will, wait!"

"I'm sorry, I have to go," I say. I don't stop. If I stop, if I talk to her, if I try to look at her and just see that blurry image instead of her actual face, I know I will implode.

• • •

I missed Thursday and Friday because of my operation, but the next morning, Monday, I have to go back to school. It's not exactly the triumphant return I had hoped for, in which I would shock my classmates with my miraculous ability to walk down the hall without a cane. No, it seems my fantasies were just that. Fantasies.

I keep my eyes closed as I walk because seeing makes me too dizzy and confused to move. I turn left, take twenty-three steps, turn right, go up the stairs, turn the corner, ascend more stairs, and walk eighteen steps toward Mrs. Everbrook's classroom. It's the same route Mr. Johnston taught me on the first day of school. That day I remember being so excited about my future as a blind student at a mainstream school. Today I feel only disappointment. It's the same school, the same route, and even essentially the same disability—I'm still legally blind, just like I used to be—but today, the walk feels completely different. Fortunately, no one at school besides the academic quiz team and Mrs. Everbrook knows I had the surgery. So they won't give my apparent postoperative blindness a second thought.

I'm sitting at my desk listening to Xander and Victoria read the announcements from the studio next door.

"And finally today," says Xander's voice from the television behind Mrs. Everbrook's desk, "we will announce the cohosts of your morning announcements show starting next semester."

His voice has all the confidence of someone whose victory is all but assured.

In all the details leading up to my surgery and then missing school last week, I forgot the winners would be named today. Great. Just what I need. A crushing defeat. On the day when I'm already totally defeated.

"And your cohosts are..."

I listen to the sound of a sealed envelope being torn open. And then silence. I strain to hear, waiting for the names. Instead there's the sound of a sheet of paper being crumpled up, and the sound of Xander's footsteps as he leaves the studio.

"Sorry about that," says Victoria calmly. She smooths out the ball of paper. "Your cohosts next semester, chosen by schoolwide vote, will be...Will and Cecily. Congratulations to the new hosts."

I'm shocked. The whole school elected us, chose us, voted for us.

After the announcements are finished, Mrs. Everbrook says, "Well, class, let's give our new cohosts a round of applause!" and I hear the patter of clapping around the room.

At the start of third period, journalism, I approach Cecily.

"I'm sorry about last night. I'm still getting used to all this," I say.

"It's fine. Take all the time you need."

"Thanks," I say. I pause, then add, "So, hey, we won."

"How about that?" she says happily.

I hold up my hand. A blur of movement suggests she's moved out hers. I bring my arm down and, in a surprising miracle of accuracy, our palms connect.

"High five," I say. "Or was that a low five? I can't really tell."

She giggles. "Wanna do something to celebrate?"

"I thought we just did," I say.

"I mean, in addition to that midlevel five," she says.

"What did you have in mind?"

"Today happens to be the last week of the van Gogh exhibit. Wanna go after school?"

"Sure," I say.

At lunch, Nick, Ion, and Whitford pile all their bodies and arms around me in a tangled hug of celebration.

"How does it feel to be a winner?" asks Ion.

"Amazing," I say, flashing a thumbs-up.

. . .

After school, Cecily takes me to the PU art museum. The security guard recognizes us.

"Back for more, huh?" he says. "You can still touch the paintings. Just make sure no one sees you."

"Actually," I say, "I had an operation. I can sort of see now."

He's momentarily speechless. "You can see?"

"Yep."

"Then why are you still wearing those glasses?"

"I can't see that great yet. Just sort of colors and shapes."

"Wow, I never heard of nothing like that."

"It's pretty rare," I say.

"Well, I'll be," he says. "I think you'll be the first blind person to ever see a van Gogh."

Cecily guides me to *Les Alyscamps,* the painting with the road in it that I touched last time, when she taught me about perspective.

"Okay," she says. "We are standing in front of it now. You can take the mask off."

I do. It's so bright in here it stings my eyes.

"What am I looking for?" I ask, trying to ignore the pain of the intense light. "How can I recognize the painting?"

"Um, it has a road, some trees—"

"Whoa, slow down. Let's start with basic shapes."

"Okay. The painting is a rectangle on the wall about ten feet in front of us. Does that help?"

"Yeah."

I search my field of vision for a rectangle. The colors shift and shimmer as I move my head.

"Ah! I think I found it!"

"Really?" she asks gleefully. "What do you see?"

"It's white, mostly. Almost entirely white. But there seem to be some colors in one part."

She sounds disappointed. "White?"

"Why? Is that wrong?"

"There's no white in *Les Alyscamps*."

"Hmmm...I don't know. I guess I'm getting my colors confused."

"Actually, maybe something else. Can you point at the edge of the painting for me?"

"I can try."

I lift a hand into my field of vision and wave it. I see a flash of white. But it's not the same as the white of the painting.

"What color is my skin?" I wonder aloud.

"Sometimes it's just called 'flesh.' But if I had to describe it, I'd say like a tan or a very light pink."

"Tan," I repeat, waving my hand.

I bring it closer to my face and see it grow larger. I can't decipher its construction; it's not shaped like any of the toy blocks I memorized yesterday. It's difficult to comprehend or describe. Apart from knowing, intellectually, that I'm holding my own hand in front of my face, I don't think I could recognize it. But still, it is fascinating. My whole life I've relied on my hands to be my eyes, my connection to the world of space. And now I can actually see them, those fingers, those tactile probes.

"Will?" says Cecily.

"Huh?"

"The painting?"

"Oh, sorry, right."

I point my hand so it lines up with one edge of the rectangle of the painting. "Here's one side." And then up. "That's the top."

"Okay, let me stop you right there," she says.

"What?"

She touches me gently. "Will, that's the *wall*. You are pointing toward the edges of the wall."

I'm puzzled. "How can you tell which is the wall and which is the painting?"

"The painting is much smaller. Here, let's walk closer."

She leads me up to the painting. And indeed, as

we draw nearer, the colors in the middle of the white rectangle—which it turns out are the painting in the center of the wall—become larger as we approach.

"Now. Can you see the road in the painting?" she asks.

I look very closely but all I see is a dance of colors. Orange, red, blue. But no road.

"It's a triangle," she hints.

"Sorry, I can't find it."

"Are your hands clean?"

"Yeah."

She lifts one of my hands and traces my fingertips across the paint.

"These are the edges of the road."

I feel the shape, and as I do, it jumps out at my eyes.

"Wow! I see it! The triangle! It's a yellow triangle, right there, a yellow triangle!"

I have no idea how a person could know this is a road, or how she would know by looking at it that this road is supposed to seem like it's getting further away on the flat canvas of the painting. But I know there's a triangle. I can see that much.

She hugs me, the protruding lens of her camera squeezing against my chest.

"Will! This is so exciting!"

Though I can't see the tears, I can hear that she starts to cry a little. "I can't believe it worked! You can see!"

"Yeah," I say. "I can."

She gushes, "I'm so happy right now. You can see! It worked! AHH! This is crazy. Here, we need a picture. A selfie of this moment. Smile!"

We stand in front of the painting, and she snaps a few photos.

Later that day, I have a follow-up appointment with Dr. Bianchi. I put on goggles and press a button when I see dots of light, and I identify colors on flash cards for him. Upon seeing me successfully recognize a color for the first time, Dr. Bianchi makes several happy exclamations in Italian and throws his hairy arms around me.

CHAPTER 21

On Tuesday evening, I'm sitting at my desk reviewing my toy blocks. I can recognize each now, almost instantly and from many angles. But after naming a shape, I still reach out and touch it to confirm I am correct.

There's a knock at my door.

It's Dad. I can tell from the knock.

"Will?"

"Come in."

He does. I turn and watch a formless, shifting array of colors as the door opens and he walks into my room and sits on the bed, the mattress exhaling under his weight.

"Seems like you've pretty much conquered those blocks now," he says.

"I guess so."

"Ready to graduate to real objects?"

I resent his implication that my progress isn't *real* because I'm learning with toys. "These are real shapes."

"Sorry, you're right. You're doing great. But now that

you know basic shapes, maybe it's time to try to identify complex ones?"

"What do you have in mind?"

"I've got a good example downstairs. You might say it's a gift to congratulate you on winning the election yesterday. Want to check it out?"

We go downstairs. I follow the sound of his movements, walking by touch with my eyes shut. But every few steps, I open my eyes for a second, take just a quick, dizzying peek at the moving hallway.

Dad says proudly, "Here it is, Will, your first complex object to identify by sight."

We are in the side hallway, which we've always kept clear of furniture. Only some photo frames hanging about shoulder level. He squares my shoulders so I'm facing the wall.

"You want me to look at the photos?" I ask. I could probably handle that. I mean, at least I now know how to tell the difference between a framed object and the wall it's hanging on.

"No, there's something else here. See if you can figure out what it is."

I wonder why Dad is doing this. Probably because I'm his son and he wants me to successfully adapt. But I can't help wondering if a part of him—maybe a part he's not even aware of—might actually want to push me to failure. He told me not to get the operation. He warned me tasks like this one would be overwhelmingly difficult. If that's the lesson he's trying to teach here, I want to prove him wrong.

So maybe this is a trick question: I'm supposed to search and search and give up, only to realize there *is* no object.

"Dad, I've walked by this wall and touched it a hundred times. There's nothing else here," I say. In other words, *I see what you're trying to do here, Dad. And I'm not amused.*

"No, I moved the object here from another part of the house."

This strikes me as suspicious. "Why not just move *me* to that part of the house?"

He chuckles. "Will, obviously if I took you to the place where this object normally is found, you would know what it is based on context. Bringing it here makes it challenging."

There's a smile in his voice. He sounds kind of excited about this "challenge" he's created for me.

But as far as teaching methods go, wouldn't it make more sense to give me some easy ones to start off with? Why not let me build my confidence by, say, going into the kitchen and finding the blender and the coffeemaker? Going into the living room and finding the TV? That kind of thing. Why deliberately make it more difficult by bringing an object out of its native habitat?

"Fine," I say with annoyance. "I'll attempt your 'challenge.'"

Instinctively, my hands draw up from my waist the way people say gunslingers draw from their holsters in Western movies.

"Sorry," I say. "Old habit."

Dad grunts something indecipherable.

I scan the wall with my eyes. It seems to be white. That's something I've learned this week: Most walls are white. I never knew that when I was blind. I guess I always thought most walls were black. Some of the kids at my old school, who weren't totally blind, told me how they'd invert the colors on their computer screens so that the background is blue or black, to make the white text and colored images easier to see. And I know people like to hang colorful decorations on their walls. So I'd always assumed they'd want black walls to make the decorations more visible. Apparently I assumed wrong.

Below the mass of white and the rectangles of the picture frames, I observe a complex, multicolored object. The shapes bounce and swirl as I try to pin them down with my gaze. I feel like I am angling my chin to look at it, which suggests it is below my eye level. So I squat. Sure enough, the object appears to grow in front of me. It's now massive and a little overwhelming. I decide to break it into its component shapes, figure them out one at a time. But whenever I identify a single shape and move on to another, I lose track of the first one and have to start all over again. It feels like when I couldn't count the dots on that die.

The task is even more difficult for me because the shapes overlap one another. Presumably if I had a better understanding of depth, I could differentiate which shape is at which depth, but because the world appears essentially flat to me, all the lines run together, crisscrossing, bending, curling over one another. Is *that* line important? How about this one? Which lines make up the most essential outline of this object?

"Want a clue?" Dad asks.

"No," I snap, sounding angrier than I intend to. I don't want to let on that his little challenge is getting to me.

When I read braille, I move from left to right. So I decide to try that method.

I step back and stare at the left side of the object. After a while, I notice a circle. It is crisscrossed with an incalculable number of lines, but there is definitely a circle around the edges. I move right from the circle to the middle of the object. That section is complete nonsense to me, all the colors and shapes stacked up on each other. I move to the right again. After a while, I notice another circle, similar to the one on the left. Two circles. One on each side.

"I've got it!" I say, jumping up, ready to prove Dad wrong with my realization. "It's a pair of glasses!"

"No, guess again," he says, disappointed.

Two circles. One on each side.

"A dumbbell? From the weight set in the basement?"

"It's much, much larger than glasses or a dumbbell."

Well, if he's trying to demonstrate that I can't judge size, he's right. I can't. Yet.

But then it hits me. Two circles. Two wheels.

"A bike!"

"Yes!" he exclaims, clapping me on the shoulder. "A bike!"

I reach out and touch the circles, and the rubber treads light up for me: *Tires,* say my fingers. I run my hands along the center, and it names itself: *Metal bike frame.*

"You probably thought—" I begin to lash out at him for his attempt to stump me, but he interrupts.

"It's for you!"

"What?"

"A gift! For you!" He's almost giddy now. And let me emphasize this: My father is not an emotional man. I witness him get this excited maybe once a year, like when the Tour de France is on TV or something.

"I can't even walk, Dad. Much less ride a bike," I say, confused.

"That's why I got it for you!"

"I don't get it."

"I know you can't walk by sight yet, but soon you'll be able to. And soon after that, you'll be able to ride a bike. I want you to know that I believe in you. I believe you'll one day be able to ride this thing."

I'm speechless.

"Will, I know I advised you not to get the operation.

And maybe I wasn't as supportive as I should have been. But you are braver than me, son. You are in some ways... in some ways more of a man than I am. And that's why you went through with it anyway. Now you can see. And one day, we'll go on a bike ride together."

"Thanks, Dad." It means a lot. More than I can express, or want to express.

"Think of it as an early Christmas present," he says. "Or, hey, next week is Thanksgiving. It could be a Thanksgiving present."

I add, "Guess we don't need the tandem anymore, huh?"

"Oh, no, we'll save it," he says. "One day I'll be too old to ride, and I'll need you to steer me around on the tandem! HA!" He lets out his dorky one-syllable laugh.

I can't help but laugh, too.

CHAPTER 22

On Wednesday, I ask Cecily to drive us to Mole Hill Park so I can witness my first sunset. She guides me up the million stairs, and we sit down in the grass in the same spot where we sat after the homecoming dance.

Once we are settled, I finally open my eyes and discover the usual visual mayhem—colors smashing into one another, lines colliding in a noisy fight for my attention.

"Is the sun setting yet?" I ask.

"Not yet."

"So what are we looking at here? The entire city?" I ask, blinking rapidly, as if by fluttering my eyelids I will bring the view into focus.

"Basically," she says. "It's a good panorama. I mean, it's a small city. Someday you should go up in the Hollywood Hills and look at Los Angeles at night. I've gone there with my dad before. But anyway, the diminutive skyline of Toano, Kansas, will have to do for now."

"Can we see my house?"

"No, but we can see mine."

"Really? Where?" I ask.

I've still never been to her house. So this will be my first chance to experience it, and I will have the chance to do so with *eyesight* as we sit here on this hill. I wonder if her blinds are open? I hope so. I want to be able to see in through the windows. I want to look into her room and find out how she's decorated her walls.

"Oh, it's... well, you probably wouldn't be able to see it. Don't worry about it."

"No, I *want* to."

"I know you do. But... I live in a pretty crappy house."

"I don't know what a house is supposed to look like. You could tell me it was a palace, and I wouldn't know the difference by looking at it."

"All right," she agrees. "How do I point it out to you?"

"Just wave your hand in a circle around it," I say.

"My hand? It's way smaller than my hand."

"Your house is smaller than your hand?" I ask, confused.

"Are you joking? Oh, right... perspective. Sorry," she says. "Sorry, I wasn't thinking—"

"It's fine," I say, embarrassed that I still get confused by these things.

"Well, yeah, from this distance, my house is tiny. Like a little speck. All you can see is a black dot, which is the roof."

I'm still a bit curious about whether I would be able to see through her windows, but from what she's saying, I guess the answer is no. And I don't want to ask because, well, it's impossible to make that question *not* creepy.

"No problem," I say, giving up on seeing her house, at least for now. "Besides, there's something I'd much rather look at."

"What?"

"You."

She giggles. Or coughs. Or something.

I turn my head to face her. I am kind of hoping something deep inside, like my heart or whatever, will be able to identify her through pure emotional instinct. Everything else in the world may be blurry and confusing, but her face will jump out in instant high definition, radiant with beautifully articulated and meaningful lines. But this doesn't turn out to be the case. Instead, I see only the normal ocean of shifting colors, currents of hue riding into my brain via my eyes.

"Well?" she asks quietly.

"I do see a lot of green," I say. "I guess that's the grass? Unless you are green?"

"No, I'm...not green," she says, as if it had been a serious question rather than a joke.

"Wiggle your head around so I can see it," I say.

I hear a swoosh of hair, and as I do, a swirl of colors lights up in front of me: Yellow and tan and pink and light brown...

This is Cecily. This is her face.

"Okay, I see you," I say. "Do you mind if I, um, invade your personal space?"

"Yes, you can invade my personal space."

I move toward her so her head fills most of my field of vision. She holds her breath like she's nervous.

A face is a complicated thing. Even before the operation, I appreciated that. It has many parts: rippling contours shaped by the bones underneath the skin, many small spots of hair—eyebrows, eyelashes, sometimes a beard or goatee—and so many different parts—a mouth, a nose, eyes, and ears. Of course, I can't make out any of this on Cecily. I know what each of these things would feel like if I reached out my hands and touched her. But the gaze of my eyes reveals no such detail. Just unrecognizable sensory data, a jumble of shapes and colors.

Even though I don't know how to connect this visual to the physical knowledge I have about faces, I can connect the sight to the knowledge that *this is Cecily's face.*

I reach a hand up, and it lands quietly against her cheek. With the touch of my fingers, the cheek identifies itself to me. I slide my hand over to her nose, and it immediately stands and declares, *I am a nose.* In that moment, my eyes make out a triangle of skin-colored light pink. Her nose.

I bring up my other hand and run my fingertips around her eyes, which she shuts in response to my touch.

But her eyes, those windows into the soul, as they say,

are the territory of her face I am most desperate to explore. Using my hands like two bookmarks to keep from losing my place, I put my pointer fingers on her eyebrows and my thumbs on the top of her cheekbones.

"Open your eyes," I say.

She does, and with the tactile input of my fingers around them, I am able to quickly locate the perfect green circles of her irises surrounding the deep black of her pupils, and to see all this floating in the larger white space of cornea. Around her eyes and above them, on her forehead, her skin fades into a deep purple, darker than the skin on her jaw and cheeks and nose.

The green of her dual irises have tiny flakes of yellow in them, as if sprinkled with gold. I might not be able to see through the windows of Cecily's house today, but I'll happily settle for her soul.

"Green with specks of gold."

"Yes," she says.

I see her previously white corneas turn red and feel warm moisture pool against my thumbs. I swipe my thumbs to wipe the tears, and she pulls me around the neck and buries her face against my shoulder.

CHAPTER 23

When I get home, I am still high on the ecstatic rush of being so close to Cecily's face. It almost felt like...like she wanted to touch my face, too, like maybe with her lips.

I demand that both of my parents stand in front of me for a thorough examination. I connect the field of brown on the bottom half of Dad's head with the prickly bristles of his beard. I associate the thin horizontal lines on Mom's forehead with the neat ridges of her eyebrows, but while doing so, it occurs to me I could go look in a mirror right now and find out what I look like, all of which suddenly makes me relatively uninterested in my mother.

I go to the upstairs bathroom and shut the door. It's my first time seeing a mirror. It looks much like the rest of the world—or, at least, the way I see the world—a swirl of indistinguishable colors and undifferentiated lines. But from what I understand about mirrors, I know at least some of these colors in front of my eyes are my own reflection. A reflection of my face and my body. I am standing right in front of myself.

I bob my head to try to pick out my face in the mirror by its motion, but the movement also has the unwanted side effect of shifting my field of vision. Instinct tells me to instead reach my hand to touch the surface, and I am startled when my fingers collide with the hard glass of the mirror instead of the colors and shapes it's reflecting. This strikes me as the funniest thing ever, and I burst out laughing.

Then an idea hits: perspective. If things get bigger the closer you move to them in real life, wouldn't that be true in the mirror, too? Can I just put my eyes right up to the mirror and then slowly move my head to search it?

I move my face right up to the mirror, and as I do so, I see a yellowish mass explode in the center. I whip around, closing my eyes and reaching out my hands to find what is happening in the bathroom. But there's nothing there. I turn to the mirror again and move in more slowly toward it. When my nose is up against the glass, I put my hand against my cheek, and I see a broad movement. That's when I realize: It's my face. My face is the yellowish mass. My face is what I see moving.

I find my eyes and stare into them. They are brown, as they have apparently been since the surgery. I wonder what they looked like before—"cloudy blue" or "milky blue" is how people always described them. My nose seems to be disproportionately large, which is disappointing. No one wants to discover they have a much larger nose than they expected. Or maybe that's something that always happens in mirrors, or at least when you are only a couple of inches away from one? My hair is brown and short. My forehead is wide and uniform in color. My lips are a darker shade than the rest of my face, and I remember that this color, the color of my lips, is similar to the one I noticed on the upper half of Cecily's face, around her eyes and forehead. I wonder why her skin changes color around those areas but mine does not.

Later that night, Mom asks, "Did you see Cecily's face tonight?"

"Yes."

"And?"

"And what?"

"What did you think?"

Many words comes to mind: Beautiful. Perfect. Radiant. But I don't feel like any of them are Mom's business.

"It was nice," I say flatly.

And it's for this reason—Cecily's face—that I don't wear the eye mask underneath my glasses to school on Thursday. I keep my eyes closed while I'm walking so I don't get dizzy, but I want to be able to open them during journalism class and examine her from afar for all of third period. Which is exactly what I am attempting to do, and I am reasonably certain I've finally located her when Mrs. Everbrook says, "Will?"

"Yes?"

"What do you think?"

"Um..." I consider bluffing with a vaguely generic answer ("I agree with what most people have been saying but disagree with others...") but figure Mrs. Everbrook will see through it since she was apparently able to tell that I wasn't paying attention in the first place. "Sorry, my mind was elsewhere."

"Then consider this your mind's formal invitation to rejoin the group," says Mrs. Everbrook.

But I have no interest in class. I just want to be with Cecily, just look at her, head to toe, examine every inch of her appearance. I try to pay attention to Mrs. Everbrook, but can't help searching the room at the same time with my eyes. I soon figure out how to locate Cecily's desk. She's like a magnet, drawing me in. And it's not just Cecily. How does anyone ever pay attention in school, when there are so many other wonderful and confusing images—hundreds, thousands, millions of pixels—constantly surrounding them?

I almost laugh when I hear the words in my mind: I am still referring to "them," the *sighted people*, as if they are some other group. As if I am not one of them. But I am now. I am a sighted person. It's not us versus them anymore. It's we.

But still, my performance and understanding is severely limited compared to the average person. There remains a gap. Maybe I'm not quite one of them. Not yet. And for that reason, I'm not able to pick out Cecily among the vibrating contours of the room.

Despite my inability to find her face across the room during class, I manage to catch up with Cecily after the bell rings. She walks me to the cafeteria before her next class, and we make plans to hang out after school.

With one last look at her face until the end of the day, I turn in to meet my friends for lunch. First thing after sitting down, I tell Nick, Ion, and Whitford about my quest to understand faces, and say that if they are all right with it—and I admit this is weird, so if they aren't, it's totally cool—I would like to examine each of their faces up close. But they are all quite eager, as it turns out. Maybe this is why Facebook is so popular: Deep down, everyone wants to put their face on display.

It's not only the first time that I've looked at any of their faces but also the first time I've touched them. Before today, each of them has been just a voice, a personality.

I start with Nick. I already know that the basic physical descriptions of appearance you hear about—eye and hair color—are the same for Nick and me. Brown eyes. Short brown hair. So I'm surprised to find that upon close inspection, we look quite different. Why do people limit their descriptions of a face to these few attributes when there are, seemingly, an infinite number of more interesting, more subtle differences? His nose is smaller, I think. His forehead is different from mine. Maybe its shape? Or color? I can't quite tell. But one thing I am confident of: This face is quite unlike the one I examined in the mirror last night.

Next is Whitford. From Nick's description, I know he's black. But I've never seen skin of a different color than my own. Bringing his face close to my eyes, I can immediately see the difference in pigmentation between Whitford's face and Nick's. Whitford's is obviously darker. And yet, not "black" as I've learned the color to be.

For all the attention race gets, for all the wars that have been fought over it, all the atrocities committed and hatred based on differences in skin tone over the centuries of human history, I would honestly have expected something... *more*. The contrast is obvious, yes, but the difference is marginal. The shape of his face is essentially the same as the others I've seen. Basic features—mouth, eyes, ears, nose. All there. What's the fuss about?

I wonder how this must look to the other kids in the cafeteria, if they are watching. The blind guy pulling his friends' faces right up to his unseeing eyes. Because they don't know I can see. They must think this is super weird. I mean, even *I* think it's kind of weird, and I know what's actually going on here.

Finally we get to Ion.

"I'm not wearing makeup," she warns.

"You never wear makeup," says Nick.

"I just thought he should know," she says defensively.

The main thing I notice about her, both from sight and touch, is her hair. It takes up a lot of space around her head. It is, I think, what people mean when they say "frizzy."

I also note that bringing her face near mine feels different than it did with Whitford and Nick. It feels...less appropriate. But overall, her face is similar to most other faces I've seen. Except for Cecily's.

CHAPTER 24

Thursday afternoon, Cecily and I sit on my bed to work on homework. I use my laptop, while she reads from books and writes in notepads. I scratch a few stickers on the wall and make her guess the flavors with her eyes closed.

At some point, we end up lying side by side, our faces about a hand width apart. I finally understand what it means to look "into" someone's eyes. You look *at* a face. But eyes? You look *into* them.

I double-check and confirm the existence of that darker-colored skin surrounding her eyes and stretching across her forehead.

"Hey, Ces?" I ask.

"Yeah?"

"It seems like your skin is colored differently on the top of your face. Am I seeing that right?"

Her voice shrinks. "You noticed?"

"I guess. I mean, I just don't understand what I'm looking at. Is it common? That skin color? I don't have many faces to compare yours with, so I don't really know."

She's silent for a weirdly long time.

"It's a birthmark," she finally says, in almost a whisper.

"Oh, like the one I have on my hand?" I say. "Mom always tells me about it. I'm not sure which hand it's on," I say, offering my palms.

She pauses, searching. "It's right here," she says, touching a point on my right hand.

"So does this one look like yours?" I ask.

Her voice is tense. "I guess. But mine is much bigger."

I hold my palm in front of my eyes, searching for the darker area.

I move my hand away, returning my gaze to her. Now that I know it's there, the discoloration on her face stands out. The entire top half, everything above her nose, is a dark purple. Based on my new knowledge of Skittle colors, I think the most accurate name for this particular hue would be "grape."

"Well, you're beautiful to me," I say.

I immediately regret using that word, *beautiful*. If she knows how I really feel, how I like her but can't be with her, it could get really awkward between us.

She lets out an unexpected gasp, like she just surfaced after being underwater for several minutes. "Really?"

Even if I've said more than I should have, I can't take it back without wounding her. So I agree.

"Yeah, of course. I mean, why wouldn't you be?"

"It's just…it's such a large…"

"Everyone has birthmarks, right?"

"Yeah, but mine is—"

"No big deal is what it is. A birthmark doesn't affect whether I think you're beautiful."

She's silent. I get the sense this birthmark issue is a big deal for her.

"You were worried about what I'd think when I saw it?"

"Of course."

"Why? Did you think it would change our…friendship?"

"I mean…I didn't know…"

"Jeez, I'm not that shallow. Besides, I can still barely see. I mean, you could be horribly disfigured, and I wouldn't know the difference!"

It's my go-to blindness joke, this bit about *XYZ could be right in front of my eyes, and I wouldn't know it.* But she doesn't laugh. Like she usually would.

"Lighten up, Ces." I poke her. "I mean, it's like—what do they call it?—a beauty mark?"

"I guess," she whispers.

"It's like that. This is just your beauty mark."

She doesn't say anything.

•••

Soon after she leaves, Mom calls me downstairs for dinner. Dad, apparently, had to do an emergency surgery, so

210

it's just the two of us at the table. I still eat by touch and feel, not by sight. No use making a mess.

"Mom," I say, "I have a question."

"What's that, sweetie?"

"Have you ever noticed," I say, gathering my words carefully, "that Cecily has a birthmark on her face?"

She sets down her fork. "Why do you ask?"

"Well, have you?" I press.

Her voice drops. "You saw it, then?"

"So you *have* seen it?" I ask.

"Well, it's—"

"It's what?" I demand.

"It's quite, um, you know..." she stammers.

"Large?" I suggest.

"Yes, that would be one way of putting it."

I think for a moment. "How common is something like that?"

"So it's a birthmark?" she asks.

"I thought you said you had seen it?" I ask.

"I *have* seen it," she says. "I just didn't know it was a birthmark, that's all."

"So how did you know what I was talking about?" I ask.

"Well, like you said, it is a rather large"—she pauses—"um, I guess the word might be disfigurement."

"Whoa, whoa, whoa," I say, feeling suddenly defensive of Cecily. "Did you seriously just call it a *disfigurement*?"

"Sorry, maybe that was the wrong word," she says.

"Why do you make it sound so negative?" I ask. "She can't help it if she was born with it."

"You're right. Sorry. I didn't mean it like that."

Annoyed, I finish my food quickly and excuse myself.

CHAPTER 25

Friday morning in journalism class, I peer out from under my sunglasses and try to look at some of the other kids sitting across the room near Cecily. It seems like the more my vision improves, the worse my eyes feel. It makes sense—it must be the demands I put on them each day as I learn to recognize more stuff. Like how I'm getting better at picking out the oval shape of faces. But again I notice that no one else looks like Cecily, with a face that's two different colors.

My entire life, people have gone out of their way to describe for me what they see. And the more unique-looking the object—be it a person, building, car, weirdly shaped chicken nugget, whatever—the more eager they are to tell me about it. So it's all the more surprising that none of my friends ever mentioned the existence of such a distinctive characteristic of Cecily's face.

Just before the bell rings, Mrs. Everbrook calls us over to her desk.

"Everything all right?" she asks. It's clear from her tone that she can tell it's not.

"Yeah, fine," I lie.

"All right," she says. "Well, since you guys will be taking over for Xander and Victoria, I wanted to remind you of our New Year's tradition. Every January, on the first day of spring semester, the coanchors share a little thought about New Year's resolutions. Nothing long, only about a minute or so. You've got plenty of time, but I thought I'd give you the heads-up so you can be thinking about what you'll say."

As we are walking out of class, Cecily asks me, "What is your resolution going to be?"

"I have no idea," I say.

● ● ●

I hurry to lunch so I can ask my friends about Cecily's birthmark. Get some answers.

"You guys remember a couple months ago, when Whitford found a chicken nugget in his lunch that looked like Jesus?" I ask.

"Yeah, that was fantastic!" says Nick, laughing at the memory.

"You all really wanted to describe it to me. How come?"

Whitford says, "You were curious as to how we could

214

all be in agreement that it looked like Jesus when no record of his appearance actually exists."

"No, I mean, before I asked about that. When you first found it on your tray, Whitford, you immediately started telling me about it. How come?"

"I guess...it was fascinating. And highly improbable. I wanted you to know about it."

"Right," I say, having made my point. "So how come you never told me about Cecily's birthmark?"

The rest of the cafeteria chatters on in the background as my friends go silent. My question hangs there, unanswered.

Finally Nick says, "See, I *told* you he was going to figure it out!"

"Figure what out?" I ask.

"That she's, you know," he says, struggling for words.

I can fill in the blank myself.

"Disfigured?" I offer, hoping they will disagree with Mom's word choice.

"No, no, no," says Nick. "It's not like that."

Okay, not disfigured. That's good. "What's it like, then?" I ask.

"She's just...um," Nick says, "not attractive in the traditional sense."

"Nick!" snaps Ion.

"What?" Nick says. "That is a polite way of putting it."

Ion exhales in frustration.

"After I had the surgery, didn't you guys know that I would see it?"

"Sure, but when we first met you, we didn't know you were eventually going to have eyesight," says Ion.

"For the record," says Nick, "I said we should have told you from the very beginning. Back when you first met her, I told Ion and Whitford that we should tell you. Like I've always said, I'm your surrogate eyes, bro."

"We weren't as tight with you back then," offers Whitford. "If it's any consolation, if you met her now, we'd definitely tell you."

"Thanks, that's a huge consolation," I say sarcastically.

"I'm just saying," replies Whitford.

"You guys always said she was really pretty," I say.

Ion says, "Of course she's pretty, Will. She's just different. You might even say, you know, special. Like, in a good way. Besides, you said it didn't matter."

"What didn't matter?" I ask.

"What she looks like. When you asked if she was pretty, I asked you if it mattered. You said no."

"It doesn't matter to what I think about her," I say. "What matters is whether you guys tell me the truth when I ask a question."

"The truth," says Ion, "is that before this year, she didn't even hang out with *us* outside of academic team practice and competitions. She's a totally different person now, and you know what? It's because of you. So why would we tell you something about her that might mess that up?"

These reasons make sense, I guess, but I am still hurt for some reason. Maybe because it feels like my friends were looking out for themselves more than me in this situation. They actually talked about telling me and then deliberately decided not to. So obviously the birthmark issue was a big deal to them, and they chose to keep it a secret. Which makes me wonder if Cecily made the same decision, and if so, why?

CHAPTER 26

Cecily drove her mom's car to school today and offers to give me a ride home. As we sit in the front seat in the school parking lot, I hear her insert the key. She turns the ignition. The engine revs a few times and sputters out.

"I'm redlining," she says with a sigh of frustration.

"What does that mean?"

"It's, like, when the gas gauge gets really low, the dial goes below this red line. It just means the tank is basically empty. We're running on fumes." She turns the key again with the same result.

"Why didn't you fill it up this morning?" I say irritably.

"Gas is expensive."

"So maybe you should've taken the bus."

She pauses. "Is there something wrong, Will?"

"Why didn't you tell me?"

"About what?"

"You know what."

"No, I don't."

She turns the key again, and the engine roars to life. I hear her shift the car from park into drive.

I think back to the Candy Land Incident. And to all the times I've ever been lied to, bullied, and tricked for being blind.

"You didn't tell me about your birthmark," I say flatly.

She puts the brakes on and shifts back into park. The engine idles, but she is silent for a moment.

"You never asked."

I say, "You should've told me before, anyway."

"Before what?"

"I don't know. Earlier on."

"Do I have a responsibility to tell you all my flaws?" she snaps. "Should I have also told you that my closet is a mess? That I broke my mom's vase when I was five years old and never told her? If you put all your flaws on display right up front, no one will ever like you."

"That's not true," I say.

"It's absolutely true, and that's why no one has ever liked me before. Because I wear my biggest flaw right on my face. It's not like I set out to trick you, Will."

"Your *biggest flaw*? So you do think it's an important part of who you are?"

"Well, of course—"

But I interrupt. "That's what I don't understand. If it's that big a deal, why wouldn't you tell me about it?"

She doesn't answer.

Eventually I ask, "But what about when I was getting the operation? Didn't you know that I would eventually be able to see you?"

"I *hoped* you would eventually be able to see me, Will."

"Then why didn't you—"

"I hoped you would be able to see me for who I am inside. I believed that you were different from everyone else. You didn't judge me for my appearance."

"So you thought I was that shallow? That just *knowing* about your birthmark would've ruined our friendship?"

"I just...didn't want to risk messing anything up between us."

A piece finally falls into place in my mind. "So the birthmark...that's why you've always been bullied?"

"Yes," she says quietly.

"And that's why you didn't want to try out for the announcements? That's why you didn't think anyone would vote for you?"

"Yes."

"Did it never occur to you that as your close friend, I might *want* to know this key bit of information so I could be there for you?"

She's silent, so I continue, "If you had just told me this one thing, I would've been able to understand. I would've understood why you thought no one liked you. I would've understood why you thought no one would want to date you. I obviously would've tried to convince you otherwise on all these things, but at least I would've known where you were coming from. These are terrible burdens you've had to carry all by yourself, Cecily. I was trying to be your friend. You know what friendship means? It means sharing the burden. You didn't have to carry it all by yourself."

She still doesn't answer.

"Well?" I say.

Finally she says, "When I first found out you were blind, it was kind of... refreshing to meet someone who didn't look at me and see my birthmark first and foremost. You saw other parts of me instead. And I liked that. I just allowed myself to enjoy it. I couldn't predict we would become this close. But after we kept hanging out, at a certain point, yeah, I felt like it had gone too far, that if I told you then, it would seem like I had taken advantage of your blindness by not telling you earlier."

When she says those words out loud, *taken advantage of your blindness,* I realize that's the other piece of why I'm so offended. It's not just knowing that she might have thought I was so shallow that I couldn't handle it, it's that she took advantage of my blindness because it happened to be more convenient. Why go through the trouble of telling the blind guy your most significant physical characteristic if you can simply allow him to stay ignorant? Why risk filling him in on what everyone else already knows when you can just leave him in the dark?

Cecily says she believed I was different from everyone

else. Well, I believed she was different, too. I believed she was the one person I could really trust. Like she might even be the one sighted person I could trust enough to be in a relationship with. But now she's thrown that all away, crumpled it up, and stomped on it.

I step out of the car and slam the door shut. I navigate back toward the school, hearing my cane *click-click-click* on the pavement as her car's idling engine fades behind me. I blink. I'm not sure if I'm blinking back tears or if I'm just blinking because my eyes feel dry.

As I walk, my mind races with questions. Do people have a duty to disclose what they look like to their blind friends? If you know someone who can't see, is there some moral obligation to tell him about any flaws in your appearance early on? Like, *Hey, I know we just met recently, but in case you ever start feeling attracted to me, you should know that for whatever reason, society wouldn't say I'm beautiful?*

Because that's all it is, right? Society or the media or whoever says people should look a certain way, and the more you deviate from that, the less beautiful you are.

But there's obviously something deeper going on with *attraction*, right? Something beyond just what society says is beautiful or not? Like, I was attracted to Cecily without ever having seen her clearly with my eyes. Because I know her. I know what she's like inside. I know how she expresses herself and the way she loves to take photos and watch sunrises, and that's what I'm attracted to.

Or at least, I thought I knew her.

The fact is, not saying what is true is the same as saying something untrue. It's a lie of omission. Cecily considered telling me the truth about herself and then decided, no, she enjoyed having a friend who didn't know what she looked like. She decided that exploiting my blindness was the best way to make me stick around, the best way to hold on to my companionship. Basically, she used my disability so she could feel better about herself.

But what hurts even more is that she assumed if I knew, I would think less of her because of something she was born with. I mean, seriously? Me, a guy who was born blind? Did she really think I was that shallow?

I liked Cecily. I really did. And if I'm being totally honest with myself, maybe someday I could've even loved her. But I don't think you can have love without trust, and I don't see how I could ever trust her again.

CHAPTER 27

I spend the weekend alone in my room, coming out only to partake in the absolute minimum levels of eating and bathroom use. I pace around, clenching and unclenching my fists, scratching random stickers with noisy aggression. Anger. Scratching. Pacing. Thoughts of Cecily, and how she withheld such a large part of herself from me when I was showing her everything. Indignation. Humiliation. More scratching. More pacing.

On Saturday, I delete all the messages I've ever posted on her wall and defriend her on Facebook. Reaching under my bed, I pull out the box of photos Cecily gave me. I march the box downstairs and dump out its contents unceremoniously on top of the food scraps in the kitchen trash can.

"What are you doing?" asks Mom suspiciously.

"Nothing," I say flatly.

Not including the angry mutterings to myself, it's the first time I've spoken all weekend.

I realize Mom is now likely to examine the contents of the trash can, so I grab a jar of mayonnaise from the fridge and pour it on top of the photos. Mom can't stand the smell of mayonnaise. That will keep her away.

On Sunday afternoon, I flop across my bed listening to music. The melody reminds me of something about Cecily, I'm not even sure what, and all of a sudden, tears roll out of my eyes. Actual tears. Hot, salty beads of confusing emotions.

At the same time I'm fuming at her, I also miss the warmth of her elbow in my hand and the scent of her body nearby as she guides me. I desperately want her in my life. But how can I be around someone who has made me so angry? Why would I *want* to be around someone like that? Does that make me crazy?

The conflict rages on for a while, and eventually my thoughts turn to my semifunctional eyes. I can only hope the tears won't hurt them. Now that I think about it, they have been hurting a little more than before. But I'm pretty sure that's been going on for several days. The physical pain and emotional pain are starting to swirl together. The eye discomfort began well before this crying episode, so I don't think the tears are doing any more damage. Other than the emotional kind. The damaged emotions that are now all that's left of what was once a friendship—and maybe a little more—with Cecily.

But as my tears start to dry up, salty on my face, they

show me something interesting. Before this weekend, I always thought my vision was kind of perpetually blurry. Turns out it was just confusing. Not blurry. The lines were actually crisp and clean; I simply didn't know what they meant. When I cry, the confusing-yet-clear world fogs over into an indecipherable mix of colors. *That's* what blurry looks like.

That's pretty much what the next four weeks feel like: blurry. I float inside a dense cloud of stormy emotions. Sometimes frustration with my limited progress, sometimes joy at how many new things I'm able to see each day. Sometimes anger at Cecily, sometimes regret about losing her. Because yeah, we don't talk anymore. It's awkward for our friends, because they can't hang out with both of us at the same time. An uneasy truce of joint friendship custody forms. She gets the friends Sunday, because I can't really play Settlers anyway. I get them Saturday. And so forth. It's weird. And sad.

• • •

Just like that, my first semester at a mainstream school is nearly over. There are two days of exams left before school lets out for winter break. After I finish on Monday, I wait for Mom to pick me up for my next therapy session with Dr. Bianchi. I've been going three times a week. Mom picks me up after school to drive me to the PU medical office building.

"How were your exams today?" Mom asks.

"Fine," I say in a tone meant to convey as little emotional revelation as possible.

"Did you see her?" she asks.

"Who?" I respond, playing dumb. This is none of Mom's business. If she really wants to know, she'll have to draw it out of me.

"Did you see *Cecily*?" she asks.

"Yeah," I say, maintaining complete flatness in my voice for each one-word sentence.

"And?" she asks.

To this I say nothing, because *and* isn't even a question.

"Well, how did it go?" she prods.

"What?" I reply.

"You and her. Was it, you know, uncomfortable?"

"No," I say. Which isn't entirely true. It was uncomfortable being in class and knowing she was in the room. It was uncomfortable walking the halls without her. But we didn't technically have any interaction, so there's nothing to measure the awkwardness by. Not with Cecily, at least. But with my friends at lunch, yeah, pretty weird. But Mom didn't ask about that, so I don't elaborate.

"Not at all?"

I say nothing, a move meant to strongly suggest this conversation is over.

Inside the medical office building, I make Mom stay in the car while I go in for the appointment. As usual.

It's been about six weeks since the second operation,

so by now I'm pretty familiar with how these sessions go. There's a lot of poking and prodding, a lot of metal gadgets that measure this or that, a lot of pinching my eyelids and lifting them off my eyes and shining a light underneath. It's a dizzying spectacle of blinking lights and spinning colors, like a rave party with an opera soundtrack.

"Any problems this week, Will?" asks Dr. Bianchi as a streak of bright white lab coat walks into the room.

"Nothing out of the ordinary," I say, assuming he is inquiring about my eyesight, not my personal life. "But I'm still having a lot of trouble with depth perception. Does that mean one of my eyes isn't working? Because don't you need both eyes to see depth?"

"Ah, yes, the depth perception. Binocular cues—that's what we call cues from using two eyes—do account for some of depth perception. But most of the cues are monocular, meaning they can be processed by a single eye."

"What are the monocular cues?" I ask.

"When one object blocks the other, it tells us it is in front. When you know the actual size of the two objects, you can compare their distance by judging their relative size and knowing the smaller one is farther away. Also, color and brightness. There are many ways."

"So I just have to keep waiting?" I say, frustrated.

"You must have patience, yes. But you must do more than simply wait. You should explore and see the new objects and places. Force your brain into unknown situations where it must comprehend the depth perception for you."

I don't know where I could find these unknown situations to put myself in. I mean, I've never even been outside Kansas. I've only left Toano for blind school and camp. My day-to-day life simply doesn't present me with many new stimuli. I mean, sure, technically everything I see is a "new" sight. But I already have route maps of school, my house, and my neighborhood in my head. So when I look at them now, I'm just connecting the objects I see with points along the paths I memorized back when I was blind. It's not actually new or unknown terrain.

"Let us now examine those eyes," he says.

We go through the usual routine. But there's one particular measurement involving a cold metal caliper pushed into the edges of my eyeballs that he performs a few more times than he usually does.

"Will, I am sorry to tell you this—I have some very bad news," he says, stepping back from the examination table where I am sitting. "Have you been experiencing blurriness around the edges of your vision? Or any pain?"

"My eyes have been feeling kind of uncomfortable lately, yes," I offer.

"As I feared."

"But I kind of had, uhhh, a relationship problem and did a lot of crying."

From his tone, I feel like it's something serious, but I

want to believe whatever problem he's found is merely a side effect of the tears.

"I'm sorry to hear that. But no, crying is not the problem. You have a buildup of fluid in your optical cavity. Very much fluid since I saw you last week," he explains.

"What does that mean?" I ask.

"Most likely, it means your body is rejecting the donor tissue."

My heart skips a beat.

"That sounds bad."

"Yes, I am afraid it is very bad."

"What will happen?" I ask.

"If it continues, all the progress we made is lost," he says, sympathy creeping into his voice.

It feels like he slapped me in the face.

"You mean I'll go back to being blind?"

He pauses. "Yes, this is what I mean."

I angle my head down toward the floor and run my fingers through my hair.

"When that—I mean, *if* that happens, couldn't you just do another transplant?"

"Unfortunately, no. Such a transplant can be performed only once. The scar tissue from the operation makes further attempts impossible."

"Well, then—I mean, there must be—is there something you can do? To stop the fluid buildup?"

"Yes, we'll of course try our best to save your eyesight.

The problem we have now is that your body identifies the new tissue in your eyes as foreign, so your own immune system tries to destroy it. This is the source of the fluid. I'm going to increase your dose of immunosuppressive drugs. But I must warn you, Will, this also puts you in danger. You must avoid contact with any person of illness, because with a compromised immune system, you are able to contract any contagious disease. You must avoid dirty or contaminated environments.

"You must not fly on airplanes, because the pressure in the airplane cabin could cause an optical rupture. No contact sports, no sudden movements. Your situation is very fragile; you must exercise great caution."

"Got it," I say, trying to sound more confident about my situation than I actually feel.

He sets a hand on my shoulder. "I'm very sorry about all this, Will. I always have the greatest hopes for you."

"What are my chances?"

"Not the best," he says, avoiding a direct answer.

"What would you say, though?" I ask. "Like a percentage?"

"That you retain the eyesight?" he says.

"Yeah," I say.

"From what I have seen today, my guess is fifty percent."

CHAPTER 28

In the car on the way home, Mom can tell there's a problem.

"What's wrong?" she asks as soon as I fasten my seat belt.

"Nothing," I say dryly.

"Honey, did Dr. Bianchi say there was something wrong?" she asks worriedly.

"No," I lie.

"Then why are you upset?"

"I'm not upset," I say, trying not to sound it.

"You're my son, Will," she says a little more gently, like she's trying to soothe me. "I can tell when you are upset."

She sounds like she's talking to a little child, which just makes everything worse. "Fine," I snap. "I'm upset. Can we go now?"

We are still parked, and she doesn't put the car in gear. Instead, she immediately asks, "Is it your eyes?"

I don't want to talk about it. I don't want her to know,

because she'll swoop into Dr. Bianchi's office and ask him a ton of questions and demand he fix me, and it will just be humiliating.

She presses again. "Will, tell me."

I don't answer. Finally I feel the car start to accelerate, and we turn out of the parking lot.

I turn my gaze out the window. I hear the sound of cars passing by, but the speeds are too fast for me to differentiate the shapes of the vehicles from the background of the road and passing buildings. What a joke that is. I want to take in the world, appreciate it all while I still can, but my eyesight just isn't good enough. So instead I get a partial glimpse through a tiny crack in the wall between the blind and the sighted, and soon that crack will seal shut completely.

Now it will be so much worse. Now I have an understanding of how much nuance I've been missing out on. I won't return to blindness with a full appreciation of what it means to see, but I *will* return with a full appreciation of what it means to be blind.

Just a few weeks ago, in fact, it seemed like I held everything that I've ever wanted in the palms of my hands. My life was on track. My plans were coming together. I had fledgling eyesight, even possible romance. But now, just like that, I've lost both. I'm left holding the empty shells of my desires, and I have to tell you, it all really sucks. Where do I go from here?

So I'm going to go back to being blind, but with a greater distrust of sighted people. How can a blind guy function without trusting others? Even with my wits and training, I still have to rely on the canes and GPS gadgets that other people make for me and sell to me, and on the occasional kindness of strangers when these things fail and I get lost.

I think for a second about how I'm supposed to share a New Year's resolution on the first day we're back at school in January. Presumably the resolution is supposed to be something, like, optimistic. But at the moment I'm feeling pretty glass-half-empty.

But hey, I've got a 50 percent chance, right? The flip of a coin. No reason not to at least *try* the meds.

"We need to stop by the pharmacy and get these new prescriptions," I tell Mom as we drive.

I hold out the prescription, and she snatches it immediately, probably taking her eyes off the road to read every bit of information she can extract. I'm sure it's a difficult task—based on what Dad always says about doctors' handwriting, I'd guess Dr. Bianchi's scribbling is about as legible to Mom as it would be to me.

The traffic slows to a stop at an intersection, giving her time to decipher the instructions. She asks, "Why are your meds changing?"

"Standard procedure after the operation," I lie.

"Hmmmmm," she says as if she's not sure she believes me.

"Can we just go to the pharmacy?" I ask impatiently.

"Of course, Will. It's right up ahead."

• • •

The next morning, the last day before winter break, it still feels weird being in the same room as Cecily during journalism class. But I'm also starting to wonder if I got angry over nothing in her car the other day. After all, I still think she's beautiful, birthmark or not. It wasn't like she set out to hurt me by deliberately deceiving me. So maybe I acted too hastily. Maybe there's still a chance to salvage this. Maybe we can at least go back to being friends. I mean, this is the last day of the fall semester. After the break, we'll become cohosts of the announcements. So it's probably time to reconcile.

As Mrs. Everbrook explains a new strategy for soliciting ad sales, I take occasional glances across the room at Cecily. I'm curious to see how she looks to me today, with this new perspective bolstering my judgment. When I look more carefully, though, I realize that I'm not looking at Cecily but at an empty desk. She's not here.

Where is she? Is everything okay? I feel a pang of jealousy, thinking about people who can covertly text under their desks.

Instead, I ask Mrs. Everbrook for a hall pass to use the restroom. I lock myself in a stall and send a text.

Ces, are you OK? Where are you?

I wait there for as long as a person could reasonably need to take care of business but get no reply.

It's agonizing waiting until lunch to ask my friends if they know why Cecily is absent.

"None of us have seen her," says Nick. "I don't think she showed up today."

"I've texted her, but she won't reply," I say, wishing for the thousandth time I could take back the words I said in the car. "Can you guys try?"

"I already did," says Ion. "She didn't reply to me, either. Whatever it is, I guess she doesn't want to talk about it."

"Hold on—maybe Mark Sybis knows. He lives next door to her," says Nick. "Yo, Mark!" he shouts, apparently to a nearby table. He speaks loudly to cut through the chatter of the cafeteria. "Have you seen Cecily?"

"Batgirl?" says a voice. "Nah, man, the car wasn't in her driveway this morning, neither."

Wait, Batgirl? Was this the guy who called Cecily Batgirl because she was walking with me in the hallway?

"Did he just call her Batgirl?" I ask, gritting my teeth.

"Yeah, I know, it's mean," says Nick. "But honestly, most of the school does it."

"Most of the school?" I say, horrified. "Just because she was hanging out with me this semester?"

"What? No," says Ion. "She's had that nickname since elementary school. I think Xander gave it to her, actually. It's because her birthmark covers the top half of her face.

Like Batman's mask. It's really mean, so we obviously never use it, but a lot of other kids do."

I swallow and find myself looking down toward the nondescript geometry of the cafeteria floor. They call her Batgirl because of the way she looks? They've been doing it since elementary school? I blink a few times in shock, and then anger. What's wrong with people? Why would anyone treat Cecily that way?

But more important right now, where is she if she's not at school and her car is gone?

"Where do you guys think she is?" I ask the table.

"Maybe she's just sick or something," suggests Whitford.

I think about our argument.

"Maybe it's my fault," I say hesitantly. "We had this big fight a few weeks ago. I said some things. . . . But since then . . ."

"What?" prompts Ion.

"I guess you could say I finally came to my senses," I say. "I really care about her. And I need her to know that."

"About time," says Ion.

"You knew?" I ask.

"About your crush? Duh," she says.

"I didn't realize it was that obvious," I say.

"It was so obvious a blind guy could've seen it," says Nick, adding, "No offense."

"Well, as soon as school's out, I'm going to find her. I've got to make things right."

"I'll drive if you want help finding her, Will."

"I'm in, too," says Ion. "But don't worry, I'm sure everything's fine."

"Like I said, maybe she's just at home sick or something," Whitford says again. "And maybe her mom just needed the car this morning. We can all go visit her after school. Let's meet in the parking lot after last period."

As it happens, I have no exam last period (gym class). Rather than leave early, though, I had planned to go see Mr. Johnston. Since it's the end of the semester, I need to go over the routes for my spring schedule with him. I don't want to ask any of my friends to do it because I feel like they're finally thinking of me as their friend first, and a visually impaired guy second, and I don't want to mess that up. I wouldn't have minded asking Cecily to help, I guess, but now she's gone.

I navigate to Mr. Johnston's office, back to that same room where I began in September. We set off immediately, starting from the main entrance once again.

"Shame about your friend Cecily," says Mr. Johnston as I'm counting out the steps in the science hallway.

I stop abruptly.

"What do you mean?" I ask.

"About her father. It seems he had a heart attack. He's home now, and he'll recover, but she went to be with him for a few weeks."

"Her father, like, in California?"

"Yes, I believe that's where he lives."

As we continue to plan out my walking routes, I'm distracted by the sensation that my chest is going to explode. I want so desperately to apologize to Cecily and to tell her I like her. But how can I now? It's impossible. Not only is she ignoring my calls and texts, it turns out she's literally a thousand miles away.

When we meet at Whitford's car after school, I fill everyone in on what I learned.

"So, Los Angeles?" says Nick.

"Yeah."

"You gonna go see her?" asks Ion.

"That would be quite the romantic gesture, but my eyes...It's a thing from the operation. I can't fly anywhere right now." I feel a knot in the back of my throat like I might cry.

"Don't give up so soon. Why don't we *drive* to Los Angeles?" Whitford suggests. "It's only, what? A couple days? And we *are* on break now."

Everyone suddenly starts talking at once, excited about Whitford's road trip. But even if we can sleep in the car, we'll still need gas money. Nick, Ion, Whitford, and I disclose our financial assets, which turn out to be less than one hundred dollars in cash between us all.

"How can *you* not have any money?" Nick asks Whitford.

"When I need money, I ask my parents, and they give it to me. It's not like I have a reason to stash it away or something."

"Well, the road trip was a nice idea," I say. "Thanks for the offer, guys."

•••

My friends drop me off at home, and I'm sitting in my room by myself when I hear Mom's footsteps on the stairs.

Then she knocks at the door. "Honey?" she calls.

"Come in."

I hear Mom walk in and feel her sit beside me on the bed.

"How're you doing?" she asks.

"Fine."

"You don't seem fine."

"Where's Dad?"

"Still at work."

She takes a breath and says, "You know, when I was growing up, my mother always told me, 'Don't marry someone you can live with. Marry someone you can't live without.'"

"Uhhh...okay," I say, unsure about the relevance of this advice to my life. "Are you and Dad getting a divorce or something?"

"Oh, no, of course not."

"So is that how you felt about Dad when you met? That you couldn't live without him?"

"Your father was...very eager to get married. We were young. And I thought he'd be able to give me the life I wanted. This house, my clothes. I didn't have all this when I was your age."

I pause, considering her answer. "Why are you telling me all this?"

"Will, honey," she says, putting a hand on my back. It feels unnatural coming from my mom, who's usually so much more, well, annoying. But I don't shrug it off. "It seemed like you were happier when you were with Cecily. In fact, I don't think I've ever seen you so happy, at least not since you were little, before you figured out that you were different from the other kids."

"Well, it's over now," I say bitterly.

"I know it's none of my business, but does it have to be?"

"Yes, actually," I say. "She left. She went to California."

"Why did she leave?"

"Her dad lives there, and he's sick. My friends and I would drive out to see her, but we can't afford it."

I wouldn't normally tell this kind of stuff to my mom, but I feel so defeated that I have no energy to keep my guard up. Plus, I want to express what I'm feeling. At the moment, Mom is the only one near enough to listen.

"I'm sorry," she says.

She really does sound sorry.

We sit in silence for a few moments, and then she leaves and I return to my staring at the ceiling. After a while—a few minutes, a few hours, who knows—I get bored and scratch a few of the stickers on the wall, noticing for the first time the colors and designs printed on each one. I text Cecily. No reply. I call her. Voice mail. As always.

It's early evening now—I can tell because the light coming through the window is all but gone—when I hear another knock on my door.

"Will?"

"Yeah, Mom?"

"Mind if I come in again?"

"Sure."

She sits down. "Here."

I reach out, and she pushes an envelope into my hand.

"Feel inside."

I open it and flip through. The bills are already stamped with braille.

"Where did you get this?"

"I sold the Tesla."

"What?" I exclaim.

"I sold it. I couldn't get top dollar on such short notice, but I have a friend from the club who I knew wanted one, and I gave her a good deal for buying it right away."

"That must be thousands of dollars.... I can't take that."

"Don't worry," she says. "I'm not giving you *all* of it. Just enough for the four of you to drive to Los Angeles and back."

"Why didn't you just go to an ATM?"

"I thought about it, but my ATM limit isn't high enough to fund a cross-country road trip. At least, not unless you were going to stay in seedy hotels and live off cheap junk food."

I still can't believe it. The Tesla was, like, her most prized possession.

"Mom, I really can't take this."

"Of course you can."

"No, really. Go get the car back. You got ripped off."

"That's why I know she won't sell it back to me. So you might as well take the money."

"What's Dad going to say?"

"Nothing if you leave before he gets home."

"Like, right now? For LA?"

"Unless you want your father grounding me *and* you."

"Um, wow...uhhhh...okay. Okay. Yeah. Let me just text my friends."

"The money comes with one stipulation."

"What's that?"

"You have to stop at the Grand Canyon on your way there. It's the most beautiful place in the world, and I want you to have the opportunity to see it."

"Mom, there's something I should tell you about my operation—"

"I already know," she says softly.

"You do?" I ask, surprised.

"There was a problem with an insurance payment, so

I had to call Dr. Bianchi's office. He mentioned the fluid buildup. Asked me how you were doing."

I'm silent for a moment. "Oh."

"That's the other reason I got rid of the Tesla. I know how upset you were about it. I'm sorry I don't always take your feelings into account. So if there's a chance you're going to return to total blindness, I've decided we shouldn't have a silent car around."

"Thanks, Mom."

"And that's also why I want you to see the Grand Canyon before it's too late. I want you to see the whole country. Now, while you still can. Can you do that for me?"

"Yeah, I will."

She kisses me on the forehead.

"This is your journey. I can't guide you anymore."

At first I think she's saying this to herself: time to let her son go. Then I realize this is the moment she was training *me* for my whole life. This is why she always insisted on guiding me instead of holding my hand when I was little—so I would be able to let go when I was ready.

"No time to waste," Mom says. "Now, get out of here before your father comes home!"

CHAPTER 29

Being in a car with other people is the opposite visual experience of being in a building with them. In a room or hallways, the background of the walls and floor remain stationary while people walk around in front. In a car, however, the heads and bodies of your fellow passengers stay still against a backdrop of constant motion as the world zooms by out the windows.

I notice this as I sit in the backseat with Nick. Ion is up front while Whitford drives.

The four of us made it out of Toano within two hours of Mom's giving me the money—an impressively quick mobilization.

We were even able to leave before Dad got back from the hospital. Our goal is to put enough distance between our homes and our hotel tonight that by the time the lies and half-truths start cracking under the scrutiny of our respective parental units, we'll be too far into our quest to turn back.

It's nighttime as we head west on Interstate 70. Most of my field of vision is dark or nearly so. I motion with my hand over light sources so Nick can identify them for me. The large but stationary glow is the dashboard. The fast-moving dots are car lights. White are headlights, red are taillights. And the tiny bluish spots overhead are stars.

"We're outside the city now, so you can see them really well here," says Nick.

Stars. Everyone talks about their beauty and ability to inspire the spirit. I roll down my window and stick my head out to gain a better view. I find a tapestry of dark sky with tiny bluish-white specks. And in between the brighter stars are many points so small and faint I can barely see them.

I bring my head back in the car.

"How many are there?" I ask, the pounding wind decreasing in volume as I roll up the window.

"Stars? I don't know," says Nick.

"I know there are like a gazillion stars in the universe."

"Sextillion," corrects Nick. "One with twenty-one zeros after it."

"Okay, but I mean just the visible stars you can see right now without a telescope or anything. Can't you just count them?"

"Uh, not really. You'd need a computer or something. There are way too many. It would be impossible to concentrate that hard."

So even for a person with normal eyesight, there's an upper limit to counting. A problem with concentrating simultaneously on the number of objects and the visual tracking of them. In fact, it's the exact same problem I have with counting, albeit with much smaller quantities.

Nick waves his hand over various constellations, which according to tradition connect together in shapes like Orion's Belt, the Big Dipper, and the Little Dipper. I can't see the images, and it's difficult for me to imagine how anyone could.

Honestly, I find more pleasure in looking at the dashboard than I do the stars. First of all, the dashboard lights are much bigger and easier to see than the stars. Second, they come in a variety of shapes. There are square buttons and several half circles. The stars, on the other hand, are only available in one model: the tiny dot. And third, unlike the monochromatic stars, the dashboard features an array of luminescent hues. Nick tries to tell me one star is actually Mars and it's red, but to me it looks like pretty much the same bluish-white as the other dots in the sky.

I think for a moment that maybe this could be the New Year's resolution I'll share on the announcements, something about appreciating all the lights and colors and sounds, about enjoying the view as we drive through life. But what is there to enjoy right now? I fell for a girl, then pushed her away. And now she's gone from my life, maybe forever. After three hours of driving, we stop in Colby,

Kansas. I shell out some twenties for two rooms at the Holiday Inn Express. There is a discussion as to how to divide sleeping arrangements; surely, we agree, Whitford's and Ion's parents would not allow them to share a room. But Nick points out that their parents aren't here, so they should do what they want. I lie in bed awake for a while thinking about Cecily, wishing there was a way to get to her faster.

The next morning we hit up the free continental breakfast in the lobby and get on the road. I have a number of missed calls on my phone from my dad last night. None, however, from Mom. I assume Dad is upset about the almost-new car being sold for a lot less than they paid for it, and about me being gone, but that Mom hasn't changed her mind about it being a good idea. So I don't call back.

As we get back on the road, I roll down the window again and look at the sky. It's quite different from last night. Where, I wonder, does the blackness go? Where do all the stars go? The galaxies have been replaced by a single star, the sun, and the black sky is now lit up in bright blue. *The color of my eyes before the operation*, I think. *The color of my eyes when I was blind.*

And there are white and blue and gray clouds of all different sizes. Unlike the stars, I find the clouds fascinating. I watch them for a full hour, during which time I see one cloud that looks like the bicycle my dad gave me the other day. Of course I know that there cannot be actual bicycles floating in the sky, and actually I have a pretty fuzzy memory about what the bike looked like, but my eyes and brain insist that yes, that's what I'm seeing. A sky bike made of clouds. It makes me laugh. My friends ask what I'm laughing about, but when I tell them, they don't find it as funny as I do.

After crossing the state line, we stop at the Colorado welcome center for a bathroom break. Nick, Whitford, and I sit on a bench inside the lobby while Ion calls her parents, who are apparently flipping out.

"Hey, Whitford," says Nick, "see that desk that says TOURIST INFORMATION?"

"Yeah."

"I'll give you a dollar if you walk over to the old lady sitting there and ask, 'Can you tell me about some of the tourists who visited here last year?'"

Whitford cracks up, and so do I.

"All the people visiting here today are, uhhhh..." I struggle to find the most appropriate word.

"Fat?" says Nick.

"Sad?" says Whitford.

"I was going to say white. Like, Caucasian. Am I seeing that correctly? I haven't noticed a single African American here."

"No, you're right," says Nick. "Not many of Whitford's kind in this part of the country."

"Kansas is five percent black," says Whitford. "We

came to Toano because PU was looking for nonwhite professors like my parents to increase its diversity. Otherwise, you can bet we'd get our black asses out of here."

"Technically, we're not in Kansas anymore," says Nick. "But Colorado has similar demographics."

"Interesting," I say.

"But, hey, that's rest stops for you. Some of the only places in America you can see a cross section of society," says Nick.

"What do you mean?" I ask.

"All the other places you go—where you live, what stores you shop at and restaurants you eat at, whether you go to public or private school—these decisions are basically determined by your family's income and socioeconomic status. But interstate rest stops are the great equalizer. From time to time we all have to drive places, and, while doing so, from time to time we all have an urgent need to take a dump."

"Going number two: the number one common denominator of America," says Whitford.

"Jeez, I step away for one second," says Ion, walking over to us, "and the conversation has already devolved into pooping?"

"Had you heard the context of our conversation," says Nick, "you would know that we were in fact analyzing important socioeconomic and racial demographic issues."

Ion snorts, unimpressed.

"How'd it go with your parents?" asks Whitford.

"Eh, okay," she says. "I think I held them off for now. They still think I'm at Kelly's house. They'll probably kill me when they find out. But let's cross that bridge when we come to it. For now, we drive!"

"You may take our lives," Nick intones loudly in a Scottish accent, "but you'll never take our freedom!"

We stand from the bench and cheer wildly.

"Is everyone looking at us now?" I ask out of the side of my mouth.

"Yeeeeeep," whispers Whitford. "Let's get out of here."

We return to I-70. I point out that I can feel us making turns as we drive, something I had not noticed in Kansas.

"Interstates in Kansas are straight and flat as far as the eye can see," says Whitford. "Colorado is more curvy."

"Kind of like your mom! Oooooooh!" says Nick. His gag, however, results in no audible fist pounds or laughs. "Nothing? Jeez. Tough crowd. Anyway, it's true. Driving across the state of Kansas is like running on a giant treadmill for eight hours."

"Can't say I've ever seen what a treadmill looks like," I say.

"Sorry, bad metaphor. The point is it's really monotonous."

I also notice a line at exactly eye level where the green of the ground and the blue of the sky intersect. This, I assume, is the horizon. But the farther we move into Colorado, the less straight this line of the horizon is.

"What's wrong with the sky?" I ask Nick.

"What do you mean?"

"There," I say, pointing my finger. "That's the horizon, right?"

"Yeah."

"It used to be a straight line. Now the sky is all bumpy."

"Those are mountains. Welcome to the Rockies."

"As in, the Rocky Mountains? But they're tiny! I thought the Rockies were supposed to be, like, huge."

"Don't worry. They'll get bigger."

It reminds me of what Cecily taught me about perspective. I guess the mountains will grow as we get closer.

Eventually I see another interruption to the horizon. But unlike the uneven bumps of the distant mountains, this is a series of parallel lines, long rectangles cut out from the blue sky. Nick tells me it is the skyscrapers of downtown Denver. My first city skyline.

As we get closer to downtown, the road becomes more crowded with cars. Eventually the buildings are so tall I have to roll down my window and stick my head out to be able to see the tops.

"The Rockies are bigger than these buildings?" I ask. "It sure doesn't look that way right now."

"Just wait. They're crazy big. You'll see," says Nick.

After we pass through Denver, I hear the engine

downshift to a lower gear and feel us angle back in a slight uphill climb. And sure enough, the mountains rise up from the horizon until they loom imposingly above the dashboard. I ask Ion to switch seats with me so I can watch them more carefully. We pull over, and I hop in front. The mountains are still only the size of my hand if I hold it close to my face, but they now take up all the background space visible beyond the front windshield, so I know they are massive. Their color is fascinating. Green along the bottom, then gray, and eventually they all turn white before tapering off into the sky.

Soon the ground around us becomes white, too.

"Is that snow?" I exclaim.

"Yep," says Whitford.

"When will we get to the top?" I ask.

"I'm not sure I-70 goes to the top of anything," says Whitford. "Roads are built on the path of least resistance, which means going in between mountains whenever possible, rather than directly over them."

"I'll look into it," says Nick, pulling out his phone.

A few minutes later, he reports, "We won't reach any summits on I-70. But we go right by Highway 40, which would take us to the top of Berthoud Pass. Elevation: eleven thousand three hundred feet."

"So it would be a detour," says Whitford, more as a statement than a question.

I share his concern. I mean, the faster we go, the sooner we find Cecily.

"How long will it take?"

"Like, an hour, tops," says Nick. "But how often do you get to be on top of the Continental Divide? If you stand there and pee in one direction, it ends up in the Atlantic Ocean, but if you turn around and pee in the other, it goes to the Pacific. How many people can say they've peed into two oceans with a single stream of urine?"

"How many people *want* to?" says Ion, clearly not convinced this would be an accomplishment.

"Will?" asks Whitford.

"Let's do it," I say. It will delay us, but I remember what my mom said about seeing everything while I still can.

"At this rate we're never going to make it to California," laments Whitford.

"Hey, it's only twenty-four hours of total driving time, and we've got two weeks off school. We're fine," says Nick.

I don't say it aloud, but the goal here is not to kill two weeks of vacation time. The goal is to find Cecily.

It's a good thing they don't give driver's licenses to people like me, because I would never be able to make sense of Highway 40. Back in Kansas, the interstate was straight and gradually tapered off into the horizon in a little point, like the street in the van Gogh painting at the museum. But Highway 40 is constantly disappearing and then reappearing after we pivot around a curve. I'm impressed with Whitford's ability to keep track of all these corners despite the many distractions—other cars whizzing by in both directions, the gigantic mountains out the windows, snow everywhere, and the fascinatingly complex dashboard in front of him.

I feel us slide a few times as we climb the road to Berthoud Pass. Whitford curses, reminding us how dangerous this is, wondering why they don't plow this more often, and suggesting we turn back. Honestly, it *does* seem dangerous. I don't know how Whitford and the other drivers can tell where the road ends and the mountain terrain begins. To me, it all just looks like one continuous plane of snow. But eventually we reach the pass and stop in a snow-covered parking lot.

The effort to step out of the car and shut the doors gets all four of us out of breath.

"The air is so thin here!" says Ion.

Every time I exhale, the mountains go dim and blurry for a second. I breathe in and out, watching the phenomenon. This, I decide, must be what people mean when they say they can "see their breath."

My friends are impressed by the view. I can tell because, well, they all shut up and just stand there for a while in the cold, no sarcastic statements or quips. And I'll admit, it is pretty cool. But to me, all views are pretty cool. To me, seeing mountains in every direction is no more and no less interesting than the circular brown hay bales that dot the endless farmlands of Kansas or the skyscraping glass towers of downtown Denver or the glowing dials of a Volvo's dashboard. But I know Cecily would appreciate this view. She'd want to see what a sunset looks like at this altitude, with this landscape.

We eventually return to I-70 and continue west. We pass three ski resorts—Copper Mountain, Vail, and Beaver Creek. From the car, the trails look like crisscrossing white lines cutting through the dark green alpine forests.

Night has fallen by the time we stop at a hotel in Grand Junction, Colorado, near the Utah border, and when I wake up in the morning, I look outside to find that I can no longer see the mountains. Have I gone nearsighted? Is this the first sign that I'm reverting to blindness?

"It's a blizzard out there," says Nick, joining me at the window. "A complete whiteout."

I hope he doesn't notice my sigh of relief.

I put on my coat and go out to stand in the thick of it, feeling the snow land on my hair, face, and outstretched hands. I hold a flake up to my eye and watch it turn to an icy-cold drop of water.

One of the main sensory cues I've always relied on is the volume of a sound. Generally speaking, the louder something is, the more significant it is. Snow is counterintuitive. It's pouring down around me so heavily that I can see no more than a few footsteps away. The snow is presumably piling up on the ground, bringing delight to skiers and despair to motorists. Berthoud Pass is probably closed. But the falling snow emits not a single note. It falls silently, it lands silently, it melts silently on my tongue.

Whitford refuses to drive while it's snowing, and we waste precious hours watching TV in the hotel until noon. Then we cross the border into Utah and head south. The terrain is different here. Gone are the mountains and foothills lined with green pine trees. The horizon is flat again, but with clusters of orange rectangles standing at right angles.

"Are those skyscrapers, too?" I ask, gesturing out the window.

"No," says Nick. "Rock formations. Most of this on our left is part of Arches National Park, actually."

It's dark outside by the time we reach Grand Canyon Village. We get two rooms at Bright Angel Lodge, and in the morning, the four of us set out for the viewing deck at the south rim of the canyon.

I still walk with my cane, but I rely on it less than I used to. I'm now able to see the ground moving beneath my feet and time it with the rhythm of my steps.

"Guys, I have a confession to make," says Nick. "I'm kind of afraid of heights."

"Awwww, poor Nick," teases Ion. "You need me to hold your hand?"

"Yeah, that's not going to happen," says Whitford.

We reach the deck, and we have to drag Nick to the edge to get him to look.

"Will's probably not afraid of heights. Are you, Will?" asks Ion.

"I don't really know. I've never looked over anything tall and steep before."

"Well, you've got a mile drop in front of you right now. Are you afraid?"

I peer over the edge, leaning on the rail.

"Can't say I feel any fear, no," I say. "It looks awesome—and I mean that in the literal sense—but I don't... the depth doesn't really register for me."

I gaze down at the canyon and out across the panorama of reds and browns. It's a feast for the eyes; that much I can understand and appreciate.

The Grand Canyon, I decide, is kind of the opposite of the Colorado Rockies. Whereas the mountains jutted above the horizon, carving triangle-shaped peaks against the blue sky, the horizon here is basically flat, with all the terrain having been chiseled out below it.

Even though she still hasn't answered my texts, I think about how I wish Cecily were with me to see this. I pull out my phone to take photos—it's a feature that I've never actually used before. My hope is that after we find her, I can show her the things we saw.

We return to the road. Our path will take us near Las Vegas, and Nick insists that we get off the interstate so I can see the Vegas strip lit up at night.

"How long will it take?" I ask. We are only hours away from Los Angeles, and the closer we get, the more eager I am to be there already.

"Will, I need you to trust me on this one. You can see

replicas of the greatest wonders of the world in Vegas," says Nick. "Stuff you'd have to travel the entire globe to see otherwise."

I hate to delay us, but it occurs to me that if my eyesight regresses, I'll never get to see *any* wonders of the world. This might be my only chance. Even if they're just replicas. But what difference does it make, if they look just like the real thing?

So I agree, and we make our way to Vegas.

He points out the attractions in front of the casinos as we drive south. First we pass two pirate ships floating in a small harbor.

"How do you know they are pirate ships and not, like, sailboats or navy vessels?" I ask.

"Those all look really different from each other. And basically all old ships look like pirate ships," he says.

At the next block we see a casino surrounded by water, like the Italian city of Venice, I'm told. Next, a casino with stone sculptures and giant pillars modeled after ancient Rome. I find the sculptures kind of creepy. To my untrained eyes, they look too much like real humans. I keep expecting them to hop down from their pedestals and start talking or walking.

One block later we reach a casino with a Paris, France, theme.

"Can you guess what that is?" asks Nick, pointing.

"The Eiffel Tower?" I ask.

"Yep. An exact replica, built at half scale."

"Wow," I say. "Probably the closest I'll ever come to seeing the real thing."

"What do you mean? Maybe you'll go to Paris someday. Who knows?"

I try to stifle a wince.

We keep driving past a casino replica of New York City. Nick points out the towers of the Empire State Building and Chrysler Building. Then we get to a half-sized model of the Statue of Liberty.

"It looks so much like the real thing that a couple years ago the US Postal Service accidentally issued a stamp with a picture of this sculpture instead of the real one in New York," said Nick. "They ended up printing billions of those stamps with the wrong statue."

"Billions?" Whitford laughs.

"For real. Look it up," says Nick.

We pass a casino shaped like a castle, and finally reach one named for a city in Egypt.

"It's a triangle," I say, thinking of Cecily.

"A pyramid, actually," says Nick. "Which is like four triangles laid—"

"I know what a pyramid *is*," I interrupt. "I just don't always recognize what I know."

"My bad. Well, here's something you probably won't recognize: In front of the pyramid is a model of the Great Sphinx."

"Half scale?"

"No, actually. This one is double the size of the original."

"How do you know all this stuff?"

"You don't get to be captain of the academic quiz team without an ability to store an endless number of useless facts."

We stay in a cheap hotel in the old downtown that night.

In the car the next morning, Ion asks, "You nervous?" Today's the day we reach LA.

"About Cecily?"

"Yeah."

"Terrified."

"I don't blame you. It's a big conversation."

"I just hope I say the right thing."

"It's not about what you say, Will."

"What's it about, then?"

"Listening."

I nod. "I guess."

She continues, "And it's a good thing you can see now, because listening is about a lot more than just what you do with your ears."

"Thanks. Just what I need. More stuff to worry about," I say.

"You'll be fine," says Ion. "Just remember: Don't talk. Listen. With your ears and your eyes and your heart."

"Don't worry, I'm already soaking up everything I can with my eyes these days."

"What do you mean?" she asks.

I look around the car. "There's something I haven't told you guys."

I close my eyes and run my fingers across my eyelids, wishing there was something I could do to get rid of the swelling behind the corneas. "My body is rejecting the transplant. There's a good chance I will go back to being blind."

"Oh, man," says Whitford.

"Will, I'm so sorry," says Ion. "What are the chances—"

"Fifty percent," I say. "A fifty-fifty chance I go back to the way I was before."

"Doesn't matter to me," says Nick.

I start to protest that it does matter quite a bit whether I can see or not, but he catches his own poor choice of words.

"Sorry, that came out wrong. What I mean is, it doesn't matter to *our friendship* whether or not you can see. We were friends before, we're friends now, we'll be friends whatever happens."

"Thanks, man," I say, reaching for his shoulder. "That means a lot."

"Who knows?" adds Nick. "If you're lucky, maybe we'll even let you join the academic quiz team."

"What? And be stuck at nerd tournaments with you losers?" I say to lighten the mood. Everyone laughs.

CHAPTER 30

We finally arrive in Los Angeles, where traffic slows us to a crawl.

"So, how exactly are we going to find her?" asks Nick.

"Cecily said her dad lived near Venice Beach. Six blocks from the ocean," I say.

"GPS can get us to Venice Beach, but that could be a lot of houses," says Nick.

"Well, I'll need your help for that," I say. "She also said it was a corner lot with a yellow house and a red surfboard on the porch. I don't think I could pick all that out from a moving car."

"No problem, we got you," says Nick.

We weave through the narrow streets of Venice Beach for about three hours. Eventually we find it. The house is such a big bright yellow that even I can see it. And once we are parked out front, I can identify the splotch of red on the porch, too.

"We'll wait out here," says Ion. "But if you need anything, we're here for you."

"I know you are," I say.

I'm able to walk without my cane, albeit slowly, across the sidewalk, through the front gate, and up to the porch. I stand there for a moment. What am I going to say? It all comes down to this. We've driven halfway across the country, and I'm standing here, and this is my one chance to apologize and win her back. I look over at my friends waiting in the car. I can't really see them, but the glance is instinctual, like I know it's what I am supposed to do. It's where I am supposed to look for support.

I knock and wait.

I hear footsteps behind the door.

Then it opens and she's standing there.

I wish I was better at reading facial expressions. Is she happy to see me? Angry? Shocked?

Knowing she's right in front of me makes me feel unsteady. I reach out a hand to grab the porch railing.

"Will?" she says, her voice registering complete confusion.

I'm not sure what I was planning to say, but I blurt out, "Ces, it's so good to see you."

I start to raise my arms to hug her but stop myself as she says, "What are you doing here?"

What am I doing here? Isn't it plainly obvious? I just drove across the country to see you, I think.

"I'm really sorry about your dad," I say.

"Thanks," she says. "It was pretty scary, but he's going

to be all right. He's even promised to start eating better and stuff."

"That's good," I say. "Yeah, really great."

"But you didn't answer my question," she says. "Why are you here? *How* are you here?"

"We drove, actually," I say. "Don't worry, not me personally. Whitford did the driving."

She doesn't laugh.

"So...?" she prompts.

Right. She still wants to know why.

Why, indeed? To answer that question could take hours. To completely explain the reason, to tell her what I've learned. But in simple terms, she *is* the reason. But she's also the one who *taught* me the reason.

See, I had been kidding myself with this idea that I needed to maintain my independence. In truth, my life has been dependent on others, or at least interdependent *with* others, since the day I was born. And my story has been woven together with Cecily's from the moment I transferred to Toano High School. She's the one who got me to try out to be cohost when I didn't think I could, who helped me scroll through the announcement script. She's filled the gaps whenever there were things I couldn't do for myself. She taught me about art, about beauty, and about sunrises. And she's filled the emotional gaps, too. Yeah, independence and self-reliance sound nice in theory, but in reality they are just synonyms for loneliness. And before

I met Cecily, I was so tired, without even realizing it, so tired of being lonely.

I think through all this, and then blurt out, "Because, Cecily, I was wrong. I always thought I could do life by myself, that I wanted to live independently. But you taught me that if there's no one to share your experiences with—if there's no one to look at the painting with, no one to audition with, no one to go to homecoming with—then what's the point?"

She's quiet for a while. "Um," she stammers.

"I love you, Cecily."

The words just come out automatically, from some truthful part of me that is finally ready to say what's inside. I don't think about them; they just happen.

She gasps. "What did you say?"

"I love you," I repeat, faster and more insistently. "I love you, Cecily."

"Will..."

But I don't care whether she loves me back, I just want her to know, right now, for this moment and to remember it always, that this is how I feel about her, and I say, "I've loved you for a long time. I loved you before I could see and after I could see. I loved you when I could only imagine your face and after I could look at your face. I love you completely, all of you."

She's quiet.

I'm breathing quickly, heavily, like I'm about to cry

or start laughing. I feel like something inside my chest—maybe my heart, or my lungs, or something—is expanding and growing, and I need her to speak before it breaks open.

"Well, say something," I plead.

"You love me?" she asks, pronouncing *love* like it's a foreign word.

My chest relaxes a little, confident she has at least gotten this message. Even if I never talk to her again after this, she'll know forever how I felt.

"Yes, I do," I say.

"Really?" But her voice breaks at the word, and she falls into my arms crying.

"What?" I ask, unsure how she's feeling.

"My whole life, I never thought—" Her voice falters but then the words spill out. "I never thought anyone would feel that way about me."

"Oh, Ces."

I wrap my arms around her and hold her face against my shoulder.

She grabs my hands.

"No cane?" she asks.

"My eyesight has improved a lot," I say.

"That's great!" she says. "Oh my God, Will, that's so great. Can you see me, like, right now?"

"Yes, I can see you quite well. You have a beautiful smile."

She bites her lip.

"I mean it," I say. "I'm sorry for the things I said in the car that day. You're beautiful. You always have been, and you always will be."

She melts against my shoulder.

"You want to go for a walk?" I ask.

"A walk?" she says, as if waking up from a dream to find us standing on a porch in California.

"I've never seen the ocean, and since we're so close, I thought, you know..."

"Okay," she says.

She takes my hand, and we walk down the stairs and back out to the sidewalk toward the beach. With my free hand, I give a little wave toward the car to let them know everything is fine. Cecily seems so wrapped up in our walk that she doesn't even notice all the thumbs-ups they flash in return.

We take off our shoes, walk out onto the sand, and eventually sit down near the water. We watch the deep green waves rise and then crash into light foam that spreads across the beach. I wonder how much longer I will be able to appreciate sights like this. I pick up a handful of sand and let it stream through my fingers. The grains are far too small to identify individually. Instead, they blend together like a streak of cream-colored paint.

"What?" she asks, grabbing my other hand. "What's wrong?"

She was so happy when the surgery seemed to have

worked, when she could finally show me a sunrise. It hurts to tell her about the swelling, but I do.

"What are the—" she starts to ask.

"Fifty percent." I say the number like I'm referring to the 50 percent chance I'll go blind again, not the 50 percent that I'll retain my eyesight.

"The flip of a coin," she says.

"The flip of a coin," I repeat.

We are quiet for a while, listening to the sound of the waves.

"So," I say, "what do we do now?"

She smiles. It feels like a misplaced expression. I wonder if I'm reading it correctly. What could she be happy about?

"You could start by kissing me," she says.

"What?" I say, caught completely off guard.

"You heard me," she says, rotating to face me.

I stammer, "I didn't realize that you felt, uh, you know, like that about me—"

She puts a finger on my lips, cutting me off. "I think I've loved you from the first time we went to that museum, Will. I just never believed you could love me back. I never believed *anyone* could love me back."

"But now?" I ask softly.

She leans her perfect face in till it's just inches away from mine. "Well, there must be some reason you drove all this way to see me, right?"

"There is," I say. "If I'm going to lose my sight again, I wanted to make sure you were the last thing I ever saw."

I put my hand behind her neck, pulling her the final inches until our lips meet. I close my eyes, and the world goes dark as my lips light up, my whole body tingling. I run my fingers up the back of her head and pull her tight against me, wanting her to know that I don't ever intend to let go. We kiss like that on the white sand beach until the sky lights up in a fiery sunset. We hold hands and watch until the sun dips below the horizon, disappearing to someplace our human eyes cannot see.

MORNING ANNOUNCEMENTS

Spring Semester, Day 1
FINAL SCRIPT
[approved for broadcast by V. Everbrook]

<u>**CECILY**</u>

Good morning, I'm Cecily Hoder.

<u>**WILL**</u>

And I'm Will Porter.

<u>**CECILY**</u>

We're your new announcement coanchors. Traditionally, this show begins each year with each host sharing his or her New Year's resolution. By the flip of a coin, Will has been chosen to go first. Will?

<u>**WILL**</u>

Thanks, Cecily.

Most of you probably know I was born blind and that I transferred here at the start of last semester. My life has changed in many unexpected ways recently, both as a result of coming to this school and because of an experimental operation I had a few months ago to potentially give me eyesight.

Today I have a wonderful girlfriend who has shown me how to appreciate the burning skies of dawn and dusk, I have parents who have patiently helped me learn shapes and colors, and I have amazing friends who have taught me to recognize everything from mountains to canyons to casinos. And as a bonus, the operation went even better than I could have hoped. My next goal is reading. By the end of the year, I hope to be reading the announcements to you off the teleprompter rather than this braille terminal. Anyway, the point I'm getting at is that my New Year's resolution is to keep my eyes and mind open. Open to beauty in all its forms. And open to all of you—my friends and classmates. Happy New Year.

AUTHOR'S NOTE

This is a story that has been growing in my mind for over a decade. I had originally imagined that Will would, after the operation, immediately be able to see the world with total understanding and comprehension. But as I researched the case histories of patients who had undergone similar procedures, I found a quite different story: Those born with total blindness have a visual cortex that developed differently from that of a sighted person, and the road to recovery is long and difficult.

The most famous (and insightful) modern case study for me was Sidney Bradford, who gained his sight at age fifty-two. His story was studied and recorded by the famous British neuropsychologist Richard Gregory. Bradford was, among other things, disappointed to discover that both he and his wife were unattractive. In fact, he found the entire world to be a visual disappointment, and as Will's dad explains in this story, Bradford's psyche fell apart and he died soon after.

The great neurologist and writer Oliver Sacks compares the Bradford case to one he followed in the 1990s in his book *An Anthropologist on Mars*. In that situation, too, the patient experienced severe depression. Eventually, his eyesight regressed to preoperative levels. But so confused and frustrated had he been by his new sense of sight that the patient was actually glad to return to blindness.

The third (and the only hopeful) case study I reviewed in depth was the book *Crashing Through* by Robert Kurson. It chronicles the story of Mike May, who is to my knowledge the only living person who had an operation to gain eyesight after living his life in total blindness and also the only person I learned of who had a successful transition, psychologically speaking, from total blindness to (some) eyesight. This can probably be attributed to his work ethic and attitude, but also, from a neurological perspective, it should be noted that May didn't lose his eyesight until age three, suggesting the possibility that he experienced some development of the visual cortex that could have aided him in his later adaptation to eyesight.

Will's procedure is based loosely on the one that May had: a stem cell transplant and then a cornea transplant.

The most extensive collection of case studies on this subject can be found in a book called *Sight Restoration After Long-term Blindness: The Problems and Behavior Patterns of Visual Rehabilitation*. It was written by an Italian named Alberto Valvo. I'm indebted to my assistant, Lisa, for tracking down a copy of this rare book at a university library.

According to Valvo, there are fewer than twenty documented cases of adults who went from total blindness to sight ever recorded in human history. Valvo says that they universally experienced depression and were often tempted after gaining eyesight to harm their eyes (or themselves).

I'm deeply indebted to all these authors, pioneers, and scientists, therefore, for giving me a framework for what it might be like for Will to gain eyesight as a teenager.

I also learned a great deal about the way the brain develops in a blind person from *Blind Vision: The Neuroscience of Visual Impairment* by Zaira Cattaneo and Tomaso Vecchi. Both of them were also kind enough to exchange several emails with me as I attempted to develop my understanding of the way Will would process the physical world—three-dimensional space, the imagination of color, etc.—without ever having seen it. They also insightfully pointed out how difficult it would be to find patients like Will to study, because people born with total blindness are exceptionally rare. Most people with visual impairments retain some of their eyesight, such as the ability to perceive light or some color, or they became blind after at least some development of the visual cortex.

Since the pioneers in this field, including Cattaneo, Vecchi, and Valvo, were all Italian, I gave Dr. Bianchi a similar ethnic heritage in their honor (although it should be noted that his grasp of the English language is far inferior to that of these scientists).

The techniques that Mrs. Chin taught Will—his ability to navigate and function in a sighted world—I myself learned through the thorough text *The Art and Science of Teaching Orientation and Mobility to Persons with Visual Impairments* by William Henry Jacobson.

As far as the writing and voice of Will, I tried to gain some understanding of the mind of a person with a visual impairment through memoirs of vision impairment, including the hilarious *Cockeyed* by Ryan Knighton, the haunting *Planet of the Blind* by Stephen Kuusisto, the poetic *Touching the Rock* by John Hull, the inspiring *Touch the Top of the World* by adventurist Erik Weihenmayer, and the wise *As I See It* by blind dynamo Tom Sullivan. I also enjoyed the classic thought-experiment novel *Blindess* by José Saramago.

I was also informed by a great many movies and documentaries about vision impairment, especially *The Eyes of Me* (which was particularly helpful in how it showed students transitioning between schools for the blind and mainstream schools and vice versa), *Going Blind, Proof, Blindsight,* and of course the Pacino classic *Scent of a Woman.*

The concept of the tyranny of the visual was first proposed by Marshall McLuhan in the 1962 book *The Gutenberg Galaxy.*

As a general note, I wish to remind the scientifically minded reader that even "normal eyesight" can sense only visible light, which itself occupies a tiny sliver of the electromagnetic spectrum. Just as a dog whistle makes a sound human ears can't detect, the vast majority of electromagnetic wavelengths—including those used for Wi-Fi, X-rays, radar, cell phones, AM/FM radio, and broadcast television—are invisible to humans, despite occupying the same spectrum as visible light. So even eyes with twenty-twenty vision are blind to well over 99 percent (assuming a linear scale) of the electromagnetic energy passing through us each and every second.

Yet even just that fraction, which we are capable of perceiving with not only our eyes but with other senses as well, contains an infinity of observable phenomena. I was inspired by that fraction to tell this story—most of us are so caught up in our personal narratives of what we have versus what we want, our little worlds of selfies and how many likes they get, that we fail to notice the beauty around us, the infinite beauty that we possess the ability to appreciate.

And although I did extensively research visual impairment and endeavor to represent it accurately in this book, I want to stress that this is fundamentally a story about how we as human beings—both the sighted and the visually impaired—sense and experience the world. It's not meant to be a scientifically accurate description of vision impairment or a textbook on the neurological development of the visual cortex. So I hope people with vision impairments will forgive the artistic liberties I've taken as a storyteller.

ACKNOWLEDGMENTS

Thanks to Ashley for encouraging me through many years of working on this, my first novel. Her enthusiasm is caffeine for the soul. Let's keep dating.

To my assistant, Lisa McLaughlin, for not only enabling me to have the time to write this book but also for tracking down an incredibly rare manuscript with historic accounts of blind adults gaining sight. I hope Dr. Bianchi is the sort of eye-care specialist you'd want to go to.

To my agent, Lucy Carson (of The Friedrich Agency), for being Will and Cecily's matchmaker. Her smart feedback on the early manuscript gave their relationship the love story it was missing. Also, thanks for all the retweets.

To my editor, Pam Gruber, who dedicated more time and attention to this book than anyone in the history of editing. Thank you. PS—I would love to see Andrew take on the academic quiz team in Settlers of Catan.

To my publicist Hallie Patterson, who continues to pitch me enthusiastically despite how many times I've mispronounced her name.

To editor-in-chief Alvina Ling, publisher Megan Tingley, and deputy publisher Andrew Smith: This house truly feels like a home. And that's because of all of you. I'm honored to be on your list.

To Leslie Shumate for consuming more than the FDA's recommended lifetime intake of cc's.

To Nichole LeFebvre for her early read. Good luck with your new literary adventure.

To my copy editors, Annie McDonnell and Ana Deboo, who astounded me with their insight. I honestly think they know more about my characters than I do.

To proofreader Tracy Koontz for creating the illusion that I'm good at words.

To Marcie Lawrence in Design, and Virginia Lawther and David Klimowicz in Production for creating something I think Will would enjoy looking at.

To global domination expert Kristin Dulaney, one of my most enthusiastic supporters from day one.

Thanks to the secret ninjas of the publishing industry, the sales team. My books are only on shelves because you fought to get them there. A bow of respect to you and to lead ninja Carol Scatorchio.

Thanks to the marketing team Stefanie Hoffman, Jennifer McClelland-Smith, Jane Lee, Victoria Stapleton, and Jenny Choy for being eager to try new ideas and for placing tremendous trust in me. I can say without an ounce of hyperbole that your level of support has exceeded my highest expectations.

And most of all, to you because you just read through a long, boring list of names. You are obviously the kind of dedicated reader for which I'm most grateful. It is because of people like you buying my books that I have the great honor of writing them.